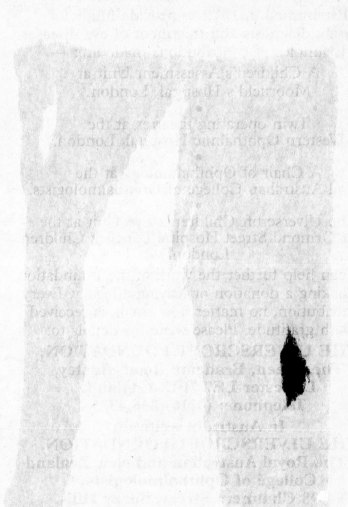

LOVE IN DISGUISE

Everyone loves to read about singer Jasmine James, but often her publicity from the press is untrue. So when she goes away for just one week's holiday in Tunisia, dressed simply and wearing a wig, can she live like other girls her age? But, while she seems to be getting away with it, her falling in love brings complications she hadn't anticipated. Will David understand why she was forced to tell so many lies to cover her tracks?

SANDRA WOOLFENDEN

◆

LOVE IN DISGUISE

Complete and Unabridged

LINFORD
Leicester

First published in Great Britain in 2011

First Linford Edition
published 2012

British Library CIP Data

Woolfenden, Sandra.
  Love in disguise. - -
  (Linford romance library)
  1. Love stories.
  2. Large type books.
  I. Title II. Series
  823.9'2–dc23

  ISBN 978–1–4448–1183–4

Published by
F. A. Thorpe (Publishing)
Anstey, Leicestershire

Set by Words & Graphics Ltd.
Anstey, Leicestershire
Printed and bound in Great Britain by
T. J. International Ltd., Padstow, Cornwall

This book is printed on acid-free paper

1

She'd done it! Through passport control in Bristol and than again on arrival at Monastir Airport in Tunisia. No comment had been made about how different she looked from her passport photo with the black wig covering her own blonde hair. When she thought about it she supposed the men and women who worked on the desks were trained to recognise people's faces and not their hair as women changed their hairstyle and colour on a regular basis. And no one on the plane had recognised her. Her friend Jan had been right.

'I'll chop off your long hair; a short hairstyle will make all the difference.'

Then when that hadn't seemed enough, Jan had loaned her the wig. She'd left the sanctuary of Jan's flat carrying a borrowed suitcase that had

1

seen better days and the contents were jeans and shorts that Jan had shopped for on her behalf plus a few T-shirts and three smarter outfits for evening on loan from her friend, but even so, not a designer label in sight.

Kelly followed the waiting rep to the designated coach and while waiting for the coach to fill up, she rang Jan.

'I've arrived,' she whispered, 'and so far, so good.'

'You'll be fine,' Jan assured her. 'Just take this week to relax and get your head sorted out.'

'Thanks Jan. Thanks for everything. Better go.'

She'd become aware of being watched by the man who'd sat next to her on the plane. She'd spoken softly but had he overheard? Her earlier thought surfaced. Was he following her? He'd attempted to strike up a conversation on the journey but she hadn't encouraged him, concentrating on the in-flight literature as though reading an engrossing novel. Had someone found out somehow that she was escaping on a package holiday and he was there to shadow her? No, she was being ridiculous. Other than Jan, absolutely no one knew where she was. Just in case, she'd have to avoid him.

It wasn't easy now though because he had taken the liberty to move seats to sit next to her again. She supposed he was good looking in a casual way with his thick brown hair and intense blue eyes. He was certainly thick-skinned. Hadn't he noticed how disinterested she was?

'Did you get through all right? Not all telephones are compatible with the networks in Tunisia.'

Did he think she'd been talking to herself? 'Yes, thank you.' Pointedly she turned away to show him she had no wish for further small talk.

The coach was dropping off at different hotels so with a little luck he'd be staying somewhere else. Unfortunately he was still there when she alighted from the coach at the last drop-off.

There was a welcome drink waiting for them at their hotel and she sat and filled in the obligatory card giving all the information required: name, passport number, reason for visit. The name on her passport was her real name, not the one splashed on the front pages of the tabloids. Despite her nerves, the girl on reception hardly looked at the card she handed over.

Still, it was a relief to be in her room away from everybody. Just get the first day over with no one guessing who she was and it would be all right. Kelly lay on her bed luxuriating in the freedom of having so much time to do absolutely nothing.

She awoke with a start, surprised she had drifted off to sleep and quickly unpacked her case and had a shower. It felt strange being on her own.

She chose the black lacy skirt Jan had loaned her together with a white blouse. She nodded to her reflection hardly recognising herself. It was a far cry from the outrageous clothes she often wore and for the first time she actually smiled, liking the simplicity of her outfit.

Kelly picked up the card that she had to take for the first evening meal, walked down the stairs instead of taking the lift, and followed people to the dining room.

The waiter smiled at her and said he hoped she would enjoy her visit to Tunisia. 'Do you mind sharing a table?' Before she had time to tell him she did, he had taken her indecision for assent and was leading her through the restaurant. 'You will sit here every evening for the meal but breakfast time sit anywhere you like.'

'Thank you,' she murmured and sat down facing her unwelcome companion from the plane.

He grinned. 'Seems we meet again. My name is David by the way.'

'Kelly,' she exchanged grudgingly.

'Most people seem to be in couples or foursomes. I expect that's why they sat us together.'

5

Was that why? Or had he bribed the waiter? It was going to be hard to avoid conversation now. Was he a reporter? She'd have to be on her guard if his questions became subtly probing. Background. Think quickly. Yes, that was it; she was a mobile hairdresser like Jan. She had borrowed Jan's clothes and now she was going to borrow her identity.

The table for two next to them was very close and the couple who sat there were probably in their late twenties Kelly worked out. They were rather tense and she wondered why. They might be thinking the same thing about her she thought. Everyone had their problems. Not David though, he appeared totally relaxed and already in a holiday mood. He introduced himself to his nearby neighbours, including her in the introduction. 'My name's David and this is Kelly.'

He made it sound as if they were a couple she thought irritably but it was easier to let it go than explain. The man smiled at David as though glad of the warm friendliness. Yes, there was definitely tension between the couple.

'My name is Leo and my wife is Sally. It's our first visit to Port el Kantaoui. We went to Hammamet on our honeymoon five years ago.'

'So this is a second honeymoon?'

'Not exactly,' Leo said.

Sally said nothing but her expression gave her away as she looked up at Leo. Kelly sensed the coolness there but David, typical man, didn't appear to notice. 'I'm sure you'll love it here,' he told Sally. 'The hotel seems very good for a start.'

'Nothing wrong with the hotel,' Sally agreed.

It's her husband that's the problem Kelly decided curiously.

'All I want to do is chill out,' Leo said. 'Sun, sand and . . . ' He smiled at Sally making a joke of it. 'Well, sun and sand anyway.'

Sally turned her attention to David. 'I've brought plenty of books with me

7

so I'll be satisfied to stretch out on a sunbed and read. I wouldn't want to be here in the middle of summer, though. May is a good month, hot but not unbearable. Have you been to Tunisia before, Kelly?'

'No, never.' I've been everywhere in Europe and America, Japan and even Russia she could have added, but didn't. And it hadn't been a holiday, just non-stop travelling. Working and travelling and then working some more. And it wasn't how she wanted her life to be.

'You need to slow down,' the doctor had told her when she'd collapsed and she'd nodded at him gratefully.

'A couple of days,' Todd had suggested. 'Take a couple of days off and you'll be fine.'

Only she wouldn't be fine in a couple of days, she knew that. Her life was going in the wrong direction, round and round and round like a carousel at the fair, round and round and going nowhere, round and round faster and faster and she didn't know how to get off.

David interrupted her thoughts. 'Sally was asking if you're going to see the belly dancer this evening, Kelly.'

'I'm sorry, I was miles away. No, I'll probably have an early night.'

'Oh, do come,' Sally pleaded, 'it'd be nice to have female company.'

'Perhaps just for a little while,' she agreed. Well, why not enjoy her time while she was here? She was only twenty-three years old, after all. And David hadn't asked her any probing questions; he'd been more interested in talking about football with Leo. Okay, she wouldn't let her defences down for fear he was a reporter playing it carefully to gain her confidence, but so far she couldn't truthfully say there was any sign of it.

'I like going all inclusive,' Leo said, 'you can budget better. You don't have to carry money round with you either.'

A terrible thought hit Kelly. Yes, it was good that everything was paid for at the hotel. She'd forgotten to get her purse back when she'd given it to Jan to go shopping for her and now she didn't have her credit card with her. She did have some spare money in the pocket on the inside of her bag but it wasn't exactly a lot. How could she have been so stupid? She'd just have to manage and change the small amount of money she had into dinar. Funny feeling that, having to be careful with money.

'You're not eating much,' David remarked.

'You're making up for me,' she returned.

'I'm going to forget the diet while I'm here,' Sally added.

You get used to being careful what you eat, Kelly reflected. After a while it becomes second nature; a price you have to pay, an acceptance of what is demanded of you. Maybe tomorrow she'd try one of the sweets, they looked so delicious.

'If you've finished,' Sally said, 'let's find some good seats for the show.'

'You girls do that and we'll go and get the drinks,' Leo suggested.

'How about a cocktail, Kelly?' Sally encouraged. 'Might as well live it up as we're on holiday.'

'Sounds good. I'll have the same as Sally.'

It was as though they were already friends.

They found comfortable seats where they'd have a good view when the show commenced. It would be fun to be a spectator.

'Are you going to the rep's meeting in the morning?'

'I'll see,' Kelly hedged not knowing quite what it would entail.

'It could be interesting and you get to meet people. They'll be trying to sell you excursions but some of them are certainly worth going on.'

'I doubt I'll be going on any excursions.' Best to get it over with. 'To tell you the truth, Sally, I can't actually afford to do anything outside the hotel.'

Sally was immediately sympathetic.

'Well, not to worry, you can still enjoy being here. The beach is right outside the hotel and the sand is simply lovely. It's beautiful just to go for a walk.'

The men had arrived with the drinks and they sat chatting and waiting for the show to start. Someone was setting up a music centre and trying a few strings on his guitar. When the music started David asked her if she'd like to dance. Her earlier distrust somewhat diminished, she stood up and went into his arms. He wasn't a particularly good dancer but it hardly mattered because as others joined them there was little room and she felt dangerously comfortable with him even when he pulled her closer.

Leo had ordered fresh drinks when they went back to their table. 'I got you the same again, Kelly.'

'Thank you, it was very nice.'

'Vodka based I think,' Sally said. 'While we're here we'll have to try them all. After all, we've paid for them.'

'I don't drink much,' Kelly admitted.

And that was another truth. She'd seen enough of others relying on drink and drugs. Miss Goody Goody her supposed boyfriend Gavin had called her. She couldn't stand him. And she was allegedly madly in love with him if the tabloids were to be believed. It was all so manufactured, one publicity stunt after another.

'You need to be kept in the public eye,' her agent Todd had insisted. She'd been brainwashed into believing he knew what was best for her. She did what she was told, went along with everything he demanded. Now it was the last thing she wanted but there was no escape.

Her name had been linked to Gavin's on Todd's instruction. He was Gavin's agent as well. Gavin was pleased to be seen with her; as a relative newcomer to the crazy world of show business he revelled in the attention he was given by reporters and photographers feeding the fuel of speculation, even though she'd rejected his advances in private.

Sally was getting giggly. Her husband Leo looked at her and smiled indulgently. Kelly had taken a liking to both of them. Sally was short and a little on the plump side with long blonde hair. Her dress was bright red and a bit too tight but she wore it with an easy confidence. Leo was much taller than Sally, almost as tall as David, his hair dark and straight, and he wore glasses which he had a habit of taking off when he was talking.

He was doing that now. 'This holiday was an impulse thing. I think we both needed a break.'

Sally nodded. 'We bought this house you see. It has great potential but there is loads to do. It sounded like fun when we went into it but we are both working full-time and the renovations are costing a fortune. We found we couldn't do it all ourselves so we've had to have the builders in for some of the jobs. Even so, in the last two years all we've done is go to work and then come home and tackle the renovations. I think we were both so tired that we took it out on each other. Leo was impatient and critical and . . . '

'And you were sulky. I thought if we could just have a break, a week away to get to know each other again, it might make life better.'

'So here we are in Tunisia.' Sally laughed. 'And the new bathroom will just have to wait.'

'Good for you,' David said.

'When did you decide to come?' Leo asked David. 'Did you and Kelly plan your holiday well in advance?'

'I didn't. How about you Kelly?'

'I thought you were married,' Sally said in surprise.

'No,' Kelly told her. 'In fact we've only just met.'

'You wouldn't know; you look right together.'

Kelly shook her head at the improbability of romance. It wasn't why she was here. All she wanted was a week away from her usual existence, a time to recharge her batteries, to do the simple things like lie in the sun or walk along the beach without a camera being thrust into her face.

'Leo and I both work in an insurance office,' Sally informed her. 'That's where we met. What do you do, Kelly?'

It was as well she had thought about it previously. 'I'm a hairdresser. I've recently started up my own business as a mobile hairdresser.'

The lie came so easily she almost believed it herself.

They didn't get on to what David did because the belly dancer had arrived amid well-natured applause as she moved erotically in her scant costume, from time to time singling out individual men to tease with her swaying hips and well toned stomach much to their delight. The music was evocative, the girl young and beautiful, dark eyes flashing. She was graceful and expert at her craft.

After the performance the music switched and again she danced with David, liberated by the soft music and the unaccustomed alcohol.

Perhaps Gavin was right and she'd be better company after a drink or two. Oh yes, Gavin. Why on earth had she let herself be bullied into pretending there was something going on between them? It was absurd when she couldn't even begin to like him. Five minutes in the business and his arrogance was insufferable. The public loved him, though, and he milked the adoration they were ready to give. And as for the media, he couldn't get enough of the column inches that they were only to happy to supply.

'Make way Jasmine James,' he told her smugly, 'Gavin North is about to knock you off the number one spot. Who knows we could even do a duet together, something sultry and sexy.' Yuk!

She didn't know what he told the reporters but he must have hinted that they were about to get engaged and a hint was enough to fabricate a full blown romance. She'd complained about it to Todd but he'd only laughed. 'All publicity is good publicity, sweetie.'

Suddenly she'd had enough. From the age of twelve until now, eleven years of her life, she'd been a target for the newspapers and magazines. This isn't the real me that they portray, she'd thought desperately, and on top of that she wondered who the real me was. She was a machine who did one gig after another appearing for one night to a packed audience all over the world, a money-making machine that supported not only herself but a host of people who looked after her and made sure she did what was expected. When she'd collapsed on stage it was because she was tired, tired of never having any time to call her own, scared that somewhere along the way she had lost her youth. Her body and soul were rebelling but Gavin even capitalised over that. Her collapse he confided to reporters was due to the heartbreak she'd suffered when he broke off the engagement; the engagement that never was.

The music stopped and David led her back to their table.

'I'm really tired,' Kelly told them. 'I hope you won't think I'm rude if I go up to bed.'

Leo smiled at his wife. 'I think we'll have an early night too.'

Sally and Leo made their way to the lift but David chose to walk up the stairs with her. They were both on the second floor and his room was just a few doors away.

'See you at breakfast then,' he said as he reached his room.

She walked the short distance to her own room and fished out her mobile phone to ring Jan. Jan had bought her a new phone while she did the shopping so she could leave her phone behind, switched off. If she didn't keep ringing Jan there should be more than enough money pre-paid to last the holiday but she'd need to keep her conversations short.

'Sorry, you seem to have the wrong number,' Jan answered at last. 'My name isn't Marlene.' There was a click.

What was going on?

2

Kelly tried Jan's phone number again and this time there was the engaged tone. She tried her mobile number and that too was switched off. Why? Jan had her purse containing her debit and credit cards and she knew her pin number; she'd used it when she'd gone out and shopped for her. No, she wouldn't steal from her even if she knew her number. Jan was her best friend, the one person in the world that she could trust. Wasn't she?

'You stay here,' Jan had ordered. 'You don't want to be seen. Don't answer the door to anyone. I'll take the landline off the hook so that it won't bother you. Yes, that was it. Jan had forgotten to replace the receiver. No, that couldn't be right, the first time she'd tried Jan had answered the phone pretending to be someone called Marlene, though she knew her voice well enough to be certain it was Jan. This time it was Jan who obviously didn't want to be bothered.

Kelly thought back to when her friend was starting up her mobile hairdressers business and Kelly had wanted to buy some of her equipment as a gift. Jan had turned that down together with the no interest loan.

'I have to do this on my own. I don't want money to come between us.'

'If you ever need any help financially, Jan, promise you'll come to me.'

'I promise,' she had smiled.

Kelly settled into bed with the mystery unsolved.

She was sure she'd be mulling it over all night but she was quickly asleep and didn't wake until she heard the ringing of her phone by the side of the bed. By the time she was alert enough to pick up the receiver the line was dead. Kelly slid out of bed, crossed the room and opened the curtains to blue skies and sunshine.

Her phone rang again, this time her mobile.

'Jan!' she cried in relief. 'Was that you on the hotel phone?'

'Yes, why didn't you answer? If I ring you on your mobile it will still cost you and you don't want to run out of credit.'

'Why didn't I answer? More to the point, why didn't you? What was going on last night?'

'I couldn't. Sean was here.' Sean was her latest boyfriend Kelly recalled. 'I told him I'd no idea where you were.'

'Why would Sean be interested?'

'Everyone's interested. You're still making the headlines. Listen to this. Jasmine Jilted! Or this paper, 'I didn't mean to break her heart, Gavin North disclosed sadly'. He's giving interviews to anyone it seems, making out he finished with you and you couldn't accept it.'

'That's pathetic.'

'The thing is Kelly, a couple of weeks ago I boasted to Sean that you and I were still good friends from schooldays.

When you rang I couldn't let him know because earlier he was all for me selling my story to the press.'

'Thanks for keeping my whereabouts secret. I just need this week's break and then I'll be fine.'

'Do you realise that you've left your purse and your cards behind?'

'Yes, I do. It's a new experience for me having no money — well hardly any. I can surely manage for the week.'

'Well, next time, I'll ring your room to make sure you have enough on your phone if you need to contact me. I'd better go.'

Deciding it was a day for sunbathing Kelly put on the white bikini Jan had purchased on her behalf and slipped a pair of white shorts and a blue T-shirt on top. She hadn't slept in her wig and wished she didn't have to wear it now as it was going to feel hot.

David, Leo and Sally were sitting together talking when she went down for breakfast. Sally waved at her and without being downright ignorant she could hardly ignore them.

'Hi!' Kelly said. 'I think I overslept.'

Both men had full cooked breakfasts and Sally had settled for croissants and fig jam.

Kelly had coffee and yoghurt which was her usual breakfast.

'You'll waste away,' David told her.

'I'm not much of a breakfast eater,' Kelly defended.

'I wish I didn't like food,' Sally sighed wistfully. 'Are you coming to the rep's meeting?'

'I guess.'

She'd been worrying too much. No one had bothered her. At the rep's meeting she sat next to David. The girl running the show had auburn hair and a bubbly personality. She answered questions and gave out literature about the excursions. Maybe one day she'd come back and go on some of them. For now she'd be satisfied to read and sunbathe and maybe go for a walk along the beautiful beach.

'So if anyone would like to go on any

24

trips come and see me,' Melissa finished with a brilliant smile.

'Anything you fancy?' David asked her.

'No, you go ahead and book. I'm just here to chill out,' she said briefly.

'I'll leave it for a while,' he said. 'For the moment I'm going for a stroll. I'd appreciate some company.'

She hesitated for a second. What harm could there be in that? 'Okay.'

It wasn't far to the port and they admired the boats moored there before being enticed into one of the cafés for a long cool drink.

Afterwards they looked at the goods displayed in the shops. 'They expect you to haggle.' David grinned. 'It's a way of life here.'

Whatever the price I absolutely can't afford it, Kelly thought.

She laughed at the handsome Tunisian men who stood outside and tried to persuade them with, 'Come in my shop? Very good price, Asda price, and lovely jubbly!'

'Maybe another day!' she responded. Definitely not this holiday.

They sat on a nearby bench and watched the fountain playing.

'Do you know the first thing I noticed about you, Kelly? It was your eyes. You have beautiful eyes, unusual colour, not exactly blue, more turquoise.'

'Oh, really!' she scoffed. 'That sounds like a chat up line.'

'It wasn't meant to be, I apologise. It was merely an observation.'

'Now I feel silly. You must think me very conceited.'

'If I remember not to use any chat up lines, do you think we could be friends?' he asked.

She met the deep blue of his eyes. 'I'd like that; friends for the week that we're here.'

* * *

She was a funny girl David thought, nervous and suspicious, but very endearing. He had this weird feeling of wanting to look after her. Take this morning at the meeting for instance. Her beautiful long-lashed eyes had searched the room looking for — looking for what? Was she running from the police? Or escaping a violent relationship? Sally had mentioned to Leo that Kelly had no spending money and Leo had passed the message on to him. She'd confirmed that truth when she had shown no inclination to go on any of the excursions though she seemed interested in the information Melissa gave everybody.

It was all very intriguing. Yes, that was it, intriguing. It had nothing to do with how sweet she was, her complexion flawless and her eyes an unusual shade of deep turquoise. Okay, she was pretty, more than pretty, quite stunning really. He wanted to get to know her better. Not because she was a pleasure to look at he told himself unconvincingly, but because she needed help. He didn't normally see himself in the role of Sir Galahad but she was definitely a damsel in distress and he was coming to her aid whether she wanted it or not. Why? Simple. He wanted to solve the mystery.

'I'm going to go back to the hotel David.'

'I'll walk back with you,' he offered.

Careful or she'd have him down for a stalker, see him as a problem.

'Okay.'

She seemed more relaxed, though he wasn't sure it would last. He wanted her to feel safe and, though he wanted to hold her hand, he made no attempt to do so. He wasn't sure she'd view holding hands as friendship.

'Shall we go back to the hotel via the beach?' he suggested and she raised no objection.

They had to pass Sally and Leo who were lying around the pool soaking up the sun and Sally sat up and called to them to join them. He would have liked to keep Kelly all to himself for a little longer. He'd have to watch this uncharacteristic possessiveness.

'I've brought you a selection of novels to read, Kelly,' Sally said.

'Thanks, I didn't think to bring any with me.' She refrained from saying getting away had all been done in such a rush.

She found herself drawn to a romance, a rags-to-riches story of a girl from the slums who wanted to be a singer. It must be so different if you have to strive for success, a sense of great achievement.

It hadn't been like that for her. She knew she had a good voice but she'd not had time for burning ambition to surface at the age of twelve. It had been her mother, Zara, who'd been the driving force. How many times had she heard her mother say, 'If it hadn't been for me you'd have been a nobody! I've made huge sacrifices so you can be a success.'

These platitudes had become more frequent recently when she'd requested that her workload could be cut.

'This is a very fickle business, sweetie,' Todd had reasoned. 'We don't want your fans to be disappointed, do we? There are lots of other gifted singers longing to take your place.'

'You've had it too easy,' Zara added grimly, making her feel ungrateful and unappreciative. Winning that first talent contest when she was so young had been exciting, her first step up the ladder to stardom. Yet, it had been hard, too. She'd had to juggle schoolwork with auditions and performances and there had been the lack of social life with girls and boys her own age. It had seemed that whenever there had been a party she'd be travelling, losing contact with the girls she'd grown up with. Only Jan, her very best friend, now remained.

Now she was fed up doing whatever was expected of her. The thought also occurred to her that maybe her mother should be the grateful one. Zara repeatedly told her that her voice was from her, she'd passed on her genes and that if only she had been given the opportunities and commitment from her own mother, she herself could have been top of the charts.

'You haven't had a bad life,' Kelly had once responded. 'You had Dad.'

'A fat lot of good he was!' Zara had snorted indignantly. 'If he'd had his way you'd never have got anywhere in this business, that's for sure.'

Kelly had felt guilty that she had been at the core of the arguments her parents had had. While her mother was busy taking her up and down the country to further her singing career, her father had found someone else and divorce followed.

She still loved her father, Bob, though Zara spoke of him with contempt.

It was when Todd, who was an exceptionally forceful agent, had taken her under his wing that things really started to happen. The first thing he'd done was change her name to Jasmine

James, reinforcing her mother's ambition for her tenfold. Now fan clubs had sprung up all over the world. She had what so many girls wanted — fame and wealth. Yet here she was in Tunisia, nobody special with no money and loving every moment of it.

Leo sat up and looked at his watch. 'Time to eat again girls and boys.'

David pulled her to her feet and the four of them went to the restaurant.

★ ★ ★

They took their time over lunch and David noted that although Kelly had hardly eaten any breakfast she had settled for a salad and very little else.

'Not much of a lunch eater either,' he chastised her.

She blushed. 'I have to watch my weight.'

Did she have an eating disorder? No, she wasn't actually anorexic just very slim, verging on too thin.

'It's a holiday!' Sally put in. 'I'll go on

32

a diet when I get home but there's no point in going all inclusive and then starving yourself!'

'I'm not starving myself, I'm just careful. I was a plump teenager and had to do something about it.'

'Sally's always going on a diet.' Leo laughed. 'The thing is she's always going but never gets there.'

'You wouldn't want me to look like a stick insect, Leo!'

That was catty, David thought, believing the remark thrown at Leo but directed at Kelly was born of jealousy.

He waited for Kelly to retaliate and he could see it cross her mind, but she let the moment go and said instead, 'Maybe I'll have a dessert tonight as a special treat.'

Sally, registering Kelly's generosity, responded, 'Maybe tonight I won't have a dessert to prove I have the teeniest touch of control.'

It could have been an uncomfortable moment David calculated, but Kelly was too decent to be petty.

Again he wondered who or what was troubling her. He felt her concern as though it were his own. No, that was ridiculous! He hardly knew the girl. What was he getting himself into?

He'd come away after breaking up with his girlfriend. Lisa was a pleasant enough girl but he'd not been deeply involved. When, unbelievably, she'd flung the ultimatum at him, 'Either we get engaged and talk about getting married or it's the end of us,' he'd been glad. For months he'd been wondering how he could finish with her without seeming too brutal.

So it wasn't on the rebound that he found himself falling for the beautiful, enigmatic girl opposite him.

3

Kelly dared to leave off her wig on the third day of the holiday. It was just too hot and with her eyes hidden behind dark sunglasses she hoped she was still unrecognisable.

She was as usual late going down to breakfast and when she joined the others they looked up in surprise.

'I was wearing a wig,' she told them amid much laughter. 'I wanted to see what it was like to have long hair.'

David was stunned. 'I would never have guessed it was a wig. Are you a natural blonde?'

'Sort of but I do have highlights put in.'

'So we have to get used to the new you,' Leo said, 'or the old you.'

'It suits you,' Sally said, 'but you look very different. You remind me of someone but at the moment I can't think who it is.'

Oh dear! Was she taking too much of a chance?

The others had now accepted that Kelly only wanted a cup of coffee and yoghurt for breakfast though she was eating a little more at other meals. Todd would be angry if she put on weight on this holiday.

'We're going into the medina at Sousse,' Sally informed her. 'You will come, won't you?'

'No, you go. I'm quite happy to read my book. I'm almost at the end and I want to see what happens.'

'We're sharing a taxi so whether you come or not it will cost us the same,' Leo said.

'I did tell him you were short of money,' Sally admitted, 'but there's no shame in it — we've all been there.'

'It's just that I've left my debit and credit cards at home,' Kelly blushed.

'It won't cost much, taxis are cheap here.' David smiled. 'If it really bothers you so much you can pay me back with interest when you get home,' he joked, giving her a wink.

And she did want to go. Very much. 'You're all very kind. It's not that I can't afford anything, it really is that I left my cards behind.'

She could see they didn't actually believe her. It was funny she thought, here she was telling them the truth but they thought she was covering up her financial situation yet all the lies she'd had to tell they accepted.

★ ★ ★

Sousse was very different from Port el Kantaoui, more the real Tunisia than the tourist area where they were staying. They went into the Soula Centre and Kelly would have loved to buy presents, especially for Jan. She admired the pottery with its vivid colours and Sally asked her opinion on a hors d'oeuvre set shaped like a starfish, each of its tentacles a separate little dish.

'I love the blue one,' she said and David wanted to buy one for her which she refused insisting she had no use for one.

'I travel a lot,' she explained for once forgetting her new identity, 'and when I'm at home I live with my mother.'

'I wouldn't have thought a mobile hairdresser would do much travelling except very locally,' he frowned. 'Okay, sorry, you just don't want me to spend money on you I guess.'

'It was a nice gesture,' she replied lightly touching his arm, 'but no, I don't want you to spend money on me.'

That was close. She'd have to be more careful in future.

Leo discovered this was one place you couldn't haggle but the prices were fair and genuine.

Later they went in the nearby medina where haggling was the norm and the sellers started at a ridiculously high price and waited to be bartered down before arriving at a price agreeable to both seller and purchaser.

'Watch your purse,' Sally advised. 'Tunisia is one of the safest places in the world but you still have to be careful with all these people around.'

One thing about not having money, Kelly thought. *You can't lose it!*

Later she didn't know quite how it happened but she found herself alone. The others must have wandered ahead while she was admiring the tablecloths. It was so crowded she couldn't make out where David, Sally and Leo were. No panic she told herself, she could find her way back to the hotel if necessary. She knew it was only about five kilometres away and she could walk if necessary; walk off the extra food she was consuming.

Not having the best sense of direction she was somehow walking through narrow alleyways where people lived.

Unlike the hotel no one she met spoke English. She sensed rather than saw that she was being followed and when the Tunisian man caught up with her she didn't know whether to be glad or afraid.

'You come with me,' he told her insistently. 'You come with me to my uncle's shop.'

Fear won and she started to run, the man following close behind. He was shouting something to her but she didn't stop to hear what he had to say. All she could think was that she had to get away and the alleyways seemed to be getting narrower and narrower.

Her breath was coming in gasps but however fast she ran he was there by her side. At last she felt she could run no further and stopped, resting against a wall.

'We are almost there.' He smiled. 'You must come and sit down and drink a cup of tea, Tunisian style. Come.'

Her legs felt too weak to run any more. She needed to be calm, not panic. She must bide her time, walk away and not show how scared she felt.

'Kelly!'

It couldn't be her pursuer, he couldn't possibly know her name, but she didn't dare to turn round to see who it was.

'Kelly!'

This time she did stop because whoever it was had caught up with her and was grasping her arm.

'David!' The relief was so enormous that she went into his arms and let him hold her while her pursuer explained to David that all he had been doing was trying to get her to visit his uncle's carpet shop.

'Couldn't you see she was scared of you?' David's voice was scathing.

'I am sorry. Perhaps now you know why I was speaking to your friend you would both like to come to my uncle's shop?'

David had to laugh at the man's audacity. 'No thank you. We have to get back to our hotel for lunch.'

'Sorry to be such a nuisance,' Kelly apologised. 'I got lost.'

'In which case I'm going to hold your

hand to make sure it doesn't happen again.'

Kelly made no protest.

Leo and Sally had left to go back to the hotel and David led her out of the bustling medina.

'We could walk back,' Kelly suggested.

'We could, but I'm ready for something to eat, in which case we'll get a taxi.' He smiled at her teasingly. 'Hang the expense!'

'Don't make fun of me, David. I can't help feeling uncomfortable not being able to afford to do anything.'

'I'm not making fun of you. I just don't want you to worry about any money I spend. I'm not quite on the breadline.'

'But I'm not your responsibility.'

'Be my responsibility just for this week. I accept that when the week is up we part as though we had never met, if that is what you want.'

His hand felt large and warm covering hers. It wasn't what she

42

wanted but it was what would happen. Better that they said goodbye and she remained 'a woman of mystery' as he sometimes called her.

* * *

After lunch David suggested a walk along the beach and Kelly no longer pretended she didn't want his company.

The sand was warm and the sea refreshingly cool as they paddled along. He reached for her hand. 'Can't have you getting lost,' he whispered softly.

Sally and Leo were very nice but she treasured the time she could spend with David alone. And they were alone, no one else on the beach existed.

'I can't believe that a few days ago we didn't know each other,' David said, his hand tightening.

'I don't really know much about you.'

'Ask away!'

'Is there a girlfriend?' Now why did she have to ask that? What business was it of hers?

'Not any more. We could have drifted into marriage and finished up a divorce statistic.'

She thought of her parents. 'Marriage isn't always perfect.'

'So you don't want to get married?'

'I wouldn't say that. I would like to marry one day and have four children, well more than one anyway. I was an only child and it can be very lonely.'

'I'm nearly thirty and have a brother eighteen months older who works as a newspaper reporter.'

She felt herself stiffen. She definitely had to be careful. Too many careless words and David could be making a telephone call to his brother. She could picture the headlines. I SPENT A WEEK IN TUNISIA WITH JASMINE JAMES.

'My turn — tell me about you. Boyfriend, fiancé?'

'Neither.'

'Ever been in love?'

Now didn't count. It was just a holiday romance, not even that. David had never made any attempt to kiss her, not that she'd given him any encouragement of course. 'Not really.'

'Too busy with your career?'

'What makes you say that?' Careful.

'Your hairdressing business must take up a lot of your time.'

Oh yes, of course! 'Yes, I suppose it does.'

He could feel her clamming up again, losing her trust in him, though he couldn't think what he could have said.

He let his hand slacken and she pulled away from him and turned. 'I'll race you back to the hotel, David. The last one there gets in the drinks.'

There was a need for her to get away from him. She hadn't liked him delving into her life and he had learned very little. There was something she was hiding and it was obvious that she had no intention of letting him into her secret. She was different from any girl he had ever met before though he couldn't say quite how. He normally had little trouble in attracting the opposite sex. Yes, that was probably it. Forget the mystery bit, that could well be in his imagination. She kept him at a distance and he wasn't used to such treatment.

He'd make more headway with Melissa, the red-headed rep in the hotel. He could tell she liked him. He could show Kelly that he got more response from other women. No, why play games? It was Kelly he wanted to be with and if he wanted to spend any time with her it would have to be on her terms. He raced ahead of her so that she was following for a change.

★ ★ ★

Once back at the hotel they went to retrieve their door keys from the reception desk.

Along with her key was a note for her. 'You had a telephone call,' the man behind the desk explained.

'I think for once I'll take the lift,' Kelly said, exhausted after their run in

46

the heat. As soon as she let herself into her room she opened the note. As expected it was from Jan. 'Need to speak to you. Will ring your hotel room at 6pm, your time.'

She picked up her book and stretched out on the bed. The heroine had made it to stardom and was singing at a charity event held at Wembley Stadium amid deafening applause while her lover who was lead guitarist in a supporting band smiled at her admiringly.

Yes, he would most likely be in show business too to survive the artificial life. Even so, it didn't always work; time apart, even sparks of jealousy when one partner was more successful than the other.

True to her word Jan rang at 6pm on the dot. Kelly snatched up the phone at the first ring. 'Sorry I missed you earlier; I'd gone for a walk with David. Anything wrong?'

'You're still hitting the headlines. No one knows where you are and your mother seems on the verge of calling in the police. 'Has my daughter been kidnapped, Jasmine James's mother sobs?' That's today's headlines.'

'Oh no!' Kelly sighed.

'I think you'll have to let her know.'

'If I do she'll know I'm ringing from Tunisia.'

'Shall I do it for you?'

'No, you've done enough. I don't want you put through the third degree. I'll ring Dad and he can ring her. Dad will understand my need to get away; Mum would tell me I'm being ridiculous. Perhaps I am.'

'No, Kelly. You're entitled to have some time to yourself. Who is this David by the way?'

'He sat next to me on the plane and then the waiter put me next to him for meals. To be honest he's rather dishy.'

'Does he know who you really are?'

'Absolutely not! I told him I was a mobile hairdresser — sorry but it was the first thing that came into my head. It's not easy living a lie, though.'

'Sounds like you've really fallen for him.'

'Crazy isn't it? The thing is I know after this week I won't ever see him again. There's another problem I've discovered today. He hasn't actually told me what he does but his brother just happens to be a newspaper reporter so I think I'll have to be doubly careful. I'm just so fed up with the lack of freedom to just be me. I'd better go, give Dad a ring now.'

Bob was delighted to hear from her. 'Just a quick call Dad to let you know I am all right, in fact better than all right. I've come away for a week's holiday and I'm having a lovely time. No one has guessed who I am and I feel so free.'

'Your mother is very concerned, Kelly. You should see the stories that are going on in the paper.'

'I've heard. I want you to ring and tell her I'm all right. I don't want her to be able to trace where I am. When I come home I'll look at my life and see what I want to do. I feel very ungrateful

49

but I feel like I just want to be an ordinary girl for once.'

'I never wanted you to be a celebrity, you know that. It all happened too quickly. Money isn't everything. Did I say something funny?'

'Not exactly. It just so happens I came away without my purse or cards and it's been quite an experience. Better go. Love you.'

'Take care, Angel. It's about time you did what you want to do.'

She looked at her watch. Time for another meal. Tonight she'd treat herself to the creme caramel that was always on the sweet buffet.

Downstairs she found David in the lounge sitting sharing a drink with Melissa. Well he wasn't her personal property! An unaccustomed stab of jealousy assailed her. This was the downside to falling in love. Is that what she was doing, falling in love? Yes, she loved everything about him, cherished every moment they spent together. Only the paths of their lives went in different directions and after this week it was unlikely that she would ever see him again.

'Coming in for dinner?' Sally asked by her side. 'Or are you waiting for David to join you?'

'No, I'll come with you.' She looked across at David still talking to Melissa, unaware of her presence. 'David is apparently otherwise engaged.'

'I want to ask you a favour,' Sally said as they walked to their table.

'Of course, I'll be glad to help if I can.'

There was no time to find out what it was because David had caught up with them.

'I didn't realise the time,' he apologised.

'We saw you talking to the beautiful Melissa,' Leo teased.

'Why didn't you come over?'

'You seemed very engrossed in your conversation,' Kelly heard herself saying, trying to keep her voice as teasing as Leo's but to her consternation she sounded somewhat peeved.

'I was talking to her about the trip to El Jem. I thought it was one trip I'd like to make so have booked it.'

Kelly felt unbelievably disappointed. She had so few days left to be with David and now she'd be losing one of them.

'There aren't many places left, Leo, so if you want to go I suggest you see Melissa soon.' He looked at Kelly. 'I took the liberty of booking a seat for you.' He raised his hand as she was about to speak, the gesture speaking volumes.

She always felt guilty on such occasions but this time there was an overriding feeling of joy.

It was later that evening that Sally brought up the favour that she wanted from Kelly.

'I love your hair in that shorter style, Kelly. Would you cut mine like that for me, please?'

4

This was one possibility that Kelly had not foreseen. There was a pause while she tried to think of an excuse.

'I've got some half decent scissors,' Sally informed her. 'You don't mind me asking, do you?'

'No, of course not, Sally,' Kelly said quickly, wondering at the same time how she was going to get out of the tricky situation. 'We'll talk about it tomorrow, shall we?'

Supposing she went ahead and did what Sally asked? No, she couldn't, that would be disastrous. She'd have to think of something. Every day brought another problem to solve. That was what came of telling lies, living a double life.

Morning brought no solution. They would have a lazy day today before the excursion tomorrow. There was no avoiding Sally.

Talk your way out of this, she thought to herself when Sally asked her what time could she do her hair.

'Can I talk to you on your own?' Kelly whispered.

'Don't you want to do it?'

'It's not that . . . '

'You seem reluctant.'

They walked behind the men who were busy sorting out sunbeds.

'Do I?' Kelly took a deep breath as a streak of inspiration dawned. 'You're right in a way and I'll tell you the reasons. Your hair really suits you for a start, but more important than that, Leo won't like it. Believe me, he won't. Men love women to have long hair. In fact I'm going to grow mine about your length.' Well, that was true; she did prefer her hair longer.

'You could be right I suppose.'

'I know I'm right. Don't do it impulsively, it takes a long time to grow back. I should know.'

'Thanks.'

Kelly smiled in relief. Wait until she

told Jan she thought, choking back her laughter.

'Is something amusing you?' David asked as she lay on her sunbed. 'You keep smiling.'

'Just happy,' she murmured, wishing she could tell him the truth about her dilemma, share the joke. The trouble was he wouldn't find it funny. She'd also have to tell him that she'd been living in a web of deceit.

'I wish I could get inside that head of yours. Here, let me put some sun protection on you. You're going a lovely golden colour and we don't want you to burn.'

'What would I do without you?'

'You don't have to do without me,' he said, his voice hoarse, his hands caressing her skin.

There was an ache deep inside her, a longing to be held in his arms, to feel his mouth on hers . . .

She forced herself to move away from his touch, to sit up, to not prolong the intimacy of the moment.

'Right,' she said, her voice brisk as though she hadn't been affected by his words. 'One good turn deserves another.' She forced a lightness she didn't feel. 'Can't have you burning either, can we?'

The time was going so quickly. Sally and Leo had left it too late to be included in the excursion so she would have David to herself. Much as she liked her new friends, being with David alone was very special.

'They're playing short mat bowls in ten minutes' time,' Leo said. 'Shall we go and play? I've heard it's fun.'

'I've never played,' Kelly said but she went anyway and Leo was right it was fun. No one took it too seriously although there was lots of cheering and laughter as the two teams battled it out.

'You have to send your bowl down to try and get it near the jack, that's the little white ball,' David advised her. 'And don't hit that chunk of wood in the middle or you lose your turn.'

It was surprising how often someone

managed to hit the wood Kelly thought, not that it really mattered that much as it was all good-natured. To her relief her bowl nestled close to the jack. 'Beginner's luck,' she said modestly but she was well pleased until the opposition hit her bowl and sent it off the mat.

'That's not fair!' she cried with mock indignation.

'That's the game,' Sally advised her giggling.

More by luck than judgement Kelly finished up on the winning side and she was quite thrilled.

Every moment was so precious but time was running out. How could she say goodbye to David?

'Is anything wrong?' David asked her later that day. The four of them were sitting inside the hotel taking advantage of the air conditioning.

'No, it's a great holiday,' Kelly answered quickly.

'It's just that sometimes you seem to go off into your own world.'

'That's what happens when you men

start talking sport, especially football,' Sally explained.

Kelly looked into David's eyes. 'If you must know, I was thinking this holiday will soon be over.'

'Next time we'll come for longer.'

'Next time?' she echoed.

He smiled. 'Most definitely.'

If only!

That evening the entertainment was karaoke and some of the singing was just terrible but they applauded anyway.

'We could do a duet,' Sally suggested to her. 'Another cocktail to give me a bit of confidence . . . '

'No, sorry, I couldn't,' Kelly apologised.

'You're very shy,' Sally told her. 'I'm sure you'd be better than some of the people we've heard tonight.'

Kelly hoped she could! 'No, please, I don't want to.'

'If she doesn't want to sing then don't make her,' David said protectively.

'You go,' Leo said, 'and we'll all cheer you on.'

Sally sighed. 'Just imagine . . . just imagine being famous. I'm going to sing one of Jasmine James's songs. Are you sure you won't join me, Kelly?'

Had she guessed? Was Sally playing games with her? Her face must have betrayed her fear.

'Okay, don't get upset, Kelly. There's another karaoke on the last night, maybe then?'

Thankfully Sally had misinterpreted her panic and she certainly had no idea who she really was. She must stop being so paranoid. For this week she was free to be like everyone else here on holiday.

Sally murdered her song but Kelly clapped as loud as she could.

★　★　★

David was still wondering what Kelly's problem was. Sometimes she was happy and full of fun like she didn't have a care in the world and then in a flash her mood would change and she was like a rabbit caught in car headlights. It was as though she forgot she needed to worry and then suddenly remembered. He couldn't fathom her at all:

She was lovely to look at but didn't appear to be aware of it. There were times when he looked at her and she literally took his breath away. He wanted her with a desperation he had never known, yet at the same time felt he could destroy his chance of furthering their relationship with a careless word or action. Being close to her was a tangle of ecstasy and agony. He wanted so much to help her but for all he knew she didn't need any help. He wondered where they would be by the end of this holiday. Is that what it would be, the end; end of holiday, end of seeing her? Would she disappear from his life and leave only the agony?

Tomorrow he'd have some time with her at El Jem. It was somewhere he was interested in seeing but he couldn't even guess if she would have chosen to go if he hadn't bulldozed her into it. No, she wanted to go. She might seem easy going but he didn't think she'd do anything she didn't want to do. Even if he hadn't intervened, she would not have been persuaded to sing with Sally. She was definitely his lady of mystery.

★ ★ ★

On the coach to El Jem Kelly was sparkling with excitement. Before she'd gone to bed she'd taken one of the leaflets to read. The excursion sounded fascinating and she was with David.

As they got off the coach they were greeted by a host of street-sellers offering a concertina of postcards of the coliseum and surrounding area.

David was pleased to buy from one of them as he had forgotten to bring his camera. 'The only thing wrong with these photos,' David told her, 'is that you are not on them, though as I've discovered you hate having your photograph taken.'

She didn't answer that one. It was true, she did hate her photo taken these days as it felt like an intrusion into her life, a constant reminder that her life was not her own. Perhaps after this week she could go back to how she had once been and accept that was the price of stardom. Todd would not be pleased that she had chosen to disappear for a week but even so she had chosen a week when she would not be touring so her fans would not be disappointed. Still, she was supposed to be shortly bringing out her new release and they should have been working on it. She wasn't looking forward to seeing him. Forget that for now. She was here with David listening to what their guide had to say.

'The amphitheatre is considered amongst the most important monuments of its kind built in the Roman Empire . . .'

The way it was designed was impressive and access to the coliseum was easy. Kelly imagined 27,000 spectators there to see the gladiators fight to the death and shuddered. It was still used sometimes for classical concerts and she thought the ambience would be incredible.

'Thank you for bringing me here, David. It's been a truly wonderful day.'

'Certainly an impressive place. There's so much to see in Tunisia and we haven't even scratched the surface. Still, there's always another time.'

'Yes,' she said playing the game, 'another time.'

'I think we are calling at a museum on the way back.'

'Nothing could compare with this, though. I could stay here all day soaking up the atmosphere.'

On the coach the passengers were viewing the postcards they had bought. David had bought a replica of his own set for her and she knew she would treasure them along with the memories. He'd had good fun bartering as he was buying two and she smiled recalling how everyone had been doing the same, falling into what was expected of them in Tunisia.

The man behind was telling them what a good deal he had got. He opened up his postcards and then said angrily, 'Would you believe it! I've only got half as many as everyone else!'

There was a ripple of laughter as the story went from the front to the back of the coach. In the end the man who had been ripped off was laughing as loud as anyone else.

'Next time we'll go on the two-day safari, ride a camel and watch the sunrise,' David promised.

'Sounds wonderful,' she answered dreamily and slipped her hand into his, pretending for just a little while that when the truth came out he would somehow understand.

★   ★   ★

That evening he held her very close when they danced. She knew she was living for the moment, ignoring the future. She needed to tell him the truth, but she didn't know where to start and she feared his reaction.

'We've only two full days left,' Sally sighed when they returned to their seats. 'You can't count the last day because we'll be packing and hanging around at the airport.'

Their hotel was very comfortable and the marble floors and columns gave a feeling of coolness and space. It was far more palatial than she'd been expecting and when they'd gone walking David had insisted on taking her into other hotels that backed on to the beach for a cool drink. Every hotel was different but impressive. She felt that as a nation they must have a natural feeling for art and beauty and their architects were particularly gifted.

David agreed with her. 'That's what I do for a job; I'm an architect but I work in industry. No one is going to walk around a factory I've designed and be bowled over by the beauty.'

'Is that what you always wanted to do?'

'Yes and no. I love my job, believe it

or not, but I also like to sketch. It's my hobby though and I don't have to think I must sell a painting or I can't eat. This way I can be an artist for pleasure.'

'I'm glad we came on holiday,' Sally said as they listened to the duo playing songs from another era as though they were still in the top ten, their accents giving a special quality to the words. 'It's like stepping into a world of luxury before going back to reality.'

'Even if the new bathroom has to wait?' Leo checked.

'Even then. It's been a time to get to know each other again.'

Kelly wondered if she'd done that. She was still somewhat confused. She knew what she wanted but she couldn't have it. Because what she wanted was a chance to be like other girls her age and marry and have children and plant flowers in the garden and cook dinner for the man she loved. That man must be David though. She looked across at him and they smiled at each other. David really liked her, she knew that, but no one liked a liar and she'd told so many lies to cover up her true identity. And exactly what was her true identity? Was she Kelly or the glamorous Jasmine? Supposing David forgave her for the lies she'd needed to tell, forgave her for not being a mobile hairdresser just as long as she gave up being a singer? Could she ever stop being a singer? She was a mixture of Kelly and Jasmine, her personality split. She hated the publicity, especially the manufactured sort that was Todd's speciality, but she loved to sing.

When they went up to their rooms late that evening David walked past his own room and outside her room he took the key from her and opened the door. He had pulled her into his arms almost before the door closed.

She knew he was going to kiss her and she let it happen, more than let it happen, responded by winding her arms around his neck, raised one hand and ran it through his hair.

'If you knew how I've longed for this

moment,' David groaned.

She sighed. 'Crazy, isn't it?'

She pulled his head down to kiss her again drowning in desire, loving the closeness, the passion. He was the one to pull away and she didn't want him to, never wanted him to stop kissing her.

The next moment he had scooped her up into his arms and was laying her on the bed murmuring gentle words of endearment against her lips. They hadn't put on the light but the room was bathed in a soft glow from the moon that came through the window to make the moment perfect.

A voice in her head urged her to tell him now, tell him the truth but she couldn't. Instead she gave herself up to the ever deepening kisses.

It wasn't until he had unbuttoned her shirt to her waist that she came to her senses. There hadn't been much in the way of romance in her life. When she was nearly seventeen there had been someone she'd liked very much but it hadn't been like this. It had been pleasant she recalled and she'd enjoyed being with him. There had certainly not been this intensity. She'd been sad when he told her he'd been offered a small part in a film and was going to Hollywood but she wished him well. She'd missed him but she knew she'd not been in love with him. They still kept in contact as friends.

There had been a couple of other men she'd dated more than once but she'd never found herself in a heavy relationship.

Now here she was letting David push her shirt off her shoulders, lift her up to completely remove it, reach for the clasp of her bra while he rained gentle soothing kisses on her face, her neck . . .

'No!' she gasped. Even to her own ears it was a very weak protest, one he would ignore and she didn't know why she had said it because she didn't want him to stop. Afterwards she would tell him the truth about herself. No, she should tell him first.

'Kelly?'

'Yes.'

'It's all right. I would never take you against your will, believe me. I can wait.' He laughed softly. 'It's not easy, sweetheart, but nothing that a cold shower can't fix. I want to make love to you one day but when you're ready and it's going to be fantastic.'

'It's all right, David. I didn't mean to stop you. I want you, too.'

'Not enough,' he whispered gently.

'There's so little time.'

'Don't you believe it; I don't know what you've done, what you are scared of, but when we go home we can fight it together, you never need to be scared again.'

'It's not like you think.' Surely now was the time to explain. 'I'm not in trouble with the police . . . '

He kissed her gently. 'I'm going to say goodnight. This isn't a holiday romance or a one night stand. It won't end when we go home. You tell me your problem when you're ready. The same goes for making love. I'll even marry you first if that's what it takes. Yes, I did say that. Perhaps I should have said I love you first, but you've probably guessed that already.'

She wanted to tell him not to go but he wasn't listening and she wasn't sure whether she uttered the words or they were only in her head because he was saying goodnight and heading for the door.

Slowly she finished undressing and crept into bed wondering where they went from here. He'd told her he loved her and she knew she loved him. The short time they'd known each other didn't matter, except he didn't know her. He was in love with someone who didn't exist, someone in disguise.

5

She was shy with David next morning. He smiled at her reassuringly and she managed to smile back but her mouth quivered. When she'd woken up that morning it was like waking from a dream and she wasn't immediately sure that the previous evening had truly happened.

Sally was very quiet, looking troubled. She'd been a bit strange yesterday Kelly thought, though it wasn't until this moment that it registered. That's what comes of being so self-centred she reprimanded herself.

David and Leo were planning to watch an important football match on the big screen in the hotel that afternoon.

For once Sally only played with her breakfast. Leo seemed totally oblivious of his wife's state.

The men left them sunbathing to go and play darts and then table tennis. Kelly tried to concentrate on her book but her mind kept wandering to the previous night and she was reliving the sensation of being in David's arms. Sally was stretched out on the bed, her eyes possibly closed behind the darkness of her glasses.

'Are you all right, Sally?'

'Yes, no, I don't know . . .'

'Want to talk about it?'

'I should talk to Leo first but it's difficult.'

'Right.'

'The thing is I can't bring myself to do it, he won't be pleased; he won't be pleased at all. I don't suppose I'm making much sense. I can't expect you to understand.'

Kelly thought of her own predicament. 'I think I probably do.'

'I can't tell him yet. This holiday has been lovely; I don't want to spoil it.'

'I feel really restless lying here, Sally. Do you fancy coming for a walk?'

'No, you go, I wouldn't be very good company.'

Kelly sat up. 'All right but if you change your mind and want to talk to me in confidence I'll be back soon.'

Kelly slipped on her backless sandals and made her way through the gardens on to the beach. The water drew her to the edge and tempted her to slip off her sandals and walk through the waves, soothed by the sound and rhythm of the sea. It felt good. Last night David had declared his love for her. Whatever happened she'd remember that.

She stopped, took off the wrap she'd been wearing over her bikini and dropped it on the sand before sitting on it. She stayed there for a while listening to the sea, alone but not lonely.

'It is, isn't it? You're Jasmine James!'

The girl standing before her was gushing in her excitement and Kelly got to her feet, serenity broken. The girl was young, younger than she was herself. She mustn't panic, act calm, unconcerned; the girl was hardly likely to be a reporter.

'I can't believe it's really you!'

'Well, I'm certainly me but who do you think I am?' Kelly bluffed.

'Jasmine James of course!'

'Isn't she a singer?' Kelly asked vaguely.

The girl looked at her again, not quite so sure this time, but sure enough. 'You must be her. Okay, I can see your hair is different. Jasmine has long hair, but if you're not her you must be her double.'

Kelly stood up, peace shattered.

She started to walk back in the direction of her hotel but the girl kept with her step for step. There was no way Kelly could ignore her. 'I've been mistaken for Jasmine James before.'

'My brother is crazy about her; he has her photographs plastered all over his bedroom walls. He's not here on this holiday. I'm here with Mum and Dad and he didn't want to come away with parents so he's gone with his mates but if he'd known you were here . . . '

'Except . . . ' One more lie, how many was that? 'Except I'm not Jasmine whatever her name is.'

'What is your name?'

'Kelly.'

The girl clapped her hand over her mouth. 'That is amazing! That just happens to be Jasmine's real name too!'

'How do you know that?'

'I know everything about her. I'm not as obsessed as my brother but I do like her. She has the most fantastic voice; powerful but easy, like it's no effort. You must have heard her.'

Kelly smiled at this unknown fan while admitting to herself that she couldn't help feeling a glow from the praise. It wasn't the fans she objected to, but the publicity that Todd manufactured. 'Yes, I have heard her. What's your name by the way?'

'It's Lauren. I've got my mobile with me. Do you mind if I take your photograph to show to my brother?'

'Why do you want to do that?' Kelly asked guardedly.

Lauren giggled. 'When I go home I'm going to pretend that I met Jasmine James, make my brother wish he'd come to Tunisia.'

There could be no harm in it Kelly reflected. Lauren didn't know who she really was and there was no way she'd be informing the media. She posed obediently. It was the only way she was going to escape.

At that moment Lauren's parents came into view and Lauren called them over and introduced Kelly to them. 'Dad, you have your camera, take a photo of Kelly and me, please. When I go home I'm going to make out I met Jasmine James.'

'You could be her,' Lauren's mother said. 'Although I think you're even prettier. I don't like some of the clothes she wears, too flamboyant, but she has such an expressive voice, so strong and yet sometimes so gentle and sincere. She's most certainly my son's fantasy girl.' She gave a little gasp. 'You have a small birthmark at the top of your right arm . . .'

The whole family were staring at her in disbelief. Kelly would never have believed that even that small detail would be known. It was incredible.

'All right,' she conceded. 'I am Jasmine James. I'm on holiday, for once a private holiday. If I beg you not to give the game away . . .'

'I promise I won't say anything, well not till I go home anyway,' Lauren agreed. 'Will that do?'

Kelly nodded in relief. 'Where do you live?'

'Cardiff.'

'If you'll do that for me I'll send you tickets for the show I'm appearing in next month, the whole family including your brother as well of course.'

'Mum, have you got a pen in your bag so I can give Kelly, I mean Jasmine, our address.'

'Kelly is fine, that's what my close friends call me.'

'Just wait until I tell my mates when I get back home!'

Several photos later Kelly was free to go. She would have liked to tell David, Sally and Leo about the experience but the only person she could tell was Jan. Well, she was lucky to have got away with it for as long as she had.

It felt like she had been away from Sally for an eternity but it couldn't have been that long because the men hadn't appeared.

Sally sat up and put on her yellow top. 'Had a good walk?'

'Yes, you should have come.' Good thing she hadn't!

'I've been lying here thinking. It's driving me mad.'

'Like I said, if you want to talk to me it would be in total confidence.'

Sally took a deep breath before blurting out tearfully, 'I'm pregnant.'

'That's wonderful!'

Tears cascaded down Sally's face. 'No, it isn't. It's not part of our plan — Leo will be so angry!'

'How long have you known?'

'Since yesterday.'

'That's no time. You can't be sure.'

'Yes, I can,' Sally sobbed. 'I'm never late.' Her voice rose to a wail.

Kelly put her arm around her. 'Don't you want the baby?'

'More than anything in the world. It sounds stupid I know but I already love it. Even if it is the end of us, Leo and me, I'm going to go ahead and have the baby. I'll have to wait until I go home to tell Leo or our holiday, what's left of it, will be ruined.'

'It might not be as bad as you think,' Kelly comforted her.

'Do you think I should tell him?'

'That's up to you, but the longer you leave it the harder it gets.'

'You sound like you're talking with the voice of experience.'

'I've not been in your situation but I've told lies, not because I wanted to lie, but as a cover up. I feel like you, if I tell now it will ruin this holiday.'

'Are you talking about you and David?'

Kelly's silence was answer enough. 'You're probably blowing it up out of all proportion,' was Sally's opinion. 'Anyone can see David is besotted with you. One little lie isn't going to make any difference.'

'That's just it,' Kelly sighed, 'it's not exactly little. Once you tell a lie it takes on a life of its own and grows into a monster.'

Sally smiled at her. 'Which of us will tell first I wonder? Kelly, when we go home I hope we can still be friends. We all get on so well.'

'I'd like that. Except by then I can't see David will be in my life somehow. I suppose that's why I'm delaying telling him. Like you, I want to enjoy the little that's left of our holiday.'

Kelly looked up and saw both men approaching. Sally was right; they did all get on well. Why did life have to be so complicated?

'Did you miss us?' David asked,

sitting on Kelly's bed.

'We hardly noticed you'd gone,' Kelly replied lightly.

'Just about time for lunch.'

'All you think about is your stomach.'

'Not all I think about,' David said softly. 'You creep into my thoughts now and then.'

'I'm starving,' Leo put in. 'While you girls lazed away here, we've been burning up the calories and we need to replace them before we fade away!'

Sally joined her in orange juice with their meal. She was apparently giving the alcohol a miss.

Later they went for a walk to the port and as luck would have it passed Lauren and her parents. Lauren waved and Kelly waved back putting her fingers to her lips.

'Someone you know?' David questioned.

'Someone I met when I went for a walk this morning,' Kelly said quickly. She could have told him then, told him the truth about how she'd been recognised but somehow the lies had become second nature. Just when and how was she going to tell him?

There was the rest of the day and a full day tomorrow and then after breakfast the following day it would all be over. Perhaps tomorrow she'd tell him, hold on to the magic of being with David until then.

David had bought a book on Tunisia the day before and was actually planning their next visit.

'Once you get home you might change your mind,' Kelly said.

'Don't you want to come again? Next time we'll do a lot more sightseeing. We'll talk about a date later, and I don't want you worrying about money because I'll pay, no arguments.'

'It's not money . . . ' Tell him now; there'll never be a better opportunity.

'And you've already told me you're not running from the police. Are you married?'

'No, I'm not married. I'm not in any real relationship.'

'So, my mystery girl, it can't be anything very terrible.' He laughed.

'It's just . . . ' The words wouldn't come. David was looking at her with such love in his blue eyes, such tenderness.

He stroked her face. 'I've never felt like this about anyone before.'

'Me neither.'

'So that's all right then. I love you, you love me, nothing else matters.' His lips touched hers, gentle, undemanding.

'Hey you two lovebirds!' Leo called over. 'Sally and I are going for a stroll. You can come if you like.'

Sally's face gave across the message that she wanted to talk to Leo alone. Had she plucked up the courage to tell him about the baby?

'No, you go,' David said. 'I want to show Kelly some of the places we can visit on our next trip to Tunisia.'

Although she doubted the trip would ever happen she flicked through the pages stepping into the fantasy world again. 'I'm reading about the Berbers.

Some of them still live in caves. Can you believe that?'

'Melissa was telling me that on the excursion there is actually a chance to see how they live. That's something for next time. I thought tomorrow I'd maybe hire a car or a taxi and we could have a quick visit to Hammamet, in case you'd like to go there next time.'

'David, I . . . ' She'd tell him now before she changed her mind.

He kissed her again. 'Please, come with me. We can look at Jasmine Hammamet while we are there.'

Funny there should be a place with the same name as her stage name.

'I'll take that thoughtful look as a yes,' he told her happily. 'Jasmine Hammamet is on the outskirts of Hammamet itself; by all accounts it's rather more like being on the continent, new and pristine, not yet so popular though. You might like to go there instead.'

She made an excuse to go to her room for a shower and rang Jan.

'I'll ring you later,' Jan promised, 'I'm in the middle of a perm so I can't speak now. Some of us have to work you know. Are you all right?'

'I'm having a wonderful time except I've got myself into a right mess. I won't hold you up now. Speak to you when you have time.'

Feeling the need to speak to someone she rang her father. Bob was delighted to hear from her.

'How did Mum take my news?'

He chuckled. 'Glad you were well but rather peeved that you hadn't rung her personally. She wanted to know exactly where you were but I didn't tell her and explained that was why you'd rung me instead. I calmed her down by telling her you'd soon be home.'

'I know Todd will be furious but that doesn't worry me any more. One thing this holiday has done for me is make me feel more assertive as far as he is concerned. I am simply not going to go along with a non-stop schedule ever again. I am entitled to some private life, a real life. I'm not a child any more and it's high time he stopped treating me like one.'

'I'm glad to hear it.'

'I'd better go or I'll use up all my time on this phone.'

'Bye Angel. Enjoy the rest of your holiday.'

Yes, she thought, *that's exactly what I intend to do and let the future take care of itself.*

Feeling somewhat happier she had a long, luxurious shower, wrapped herself in a towel and wondered what she would wear out of the few choices she had. That was another thing — in future she would choose her own clothes; she didn't need to be a fashion icon. She smiled to herself. Jasmine James was about to have a makeover, stand up for herself. Todd could be as angry as he liked!

She'd washed the white blouse she'd worn on the first evening and it looked fresh and cool even without ironing. What a lot had happened since that first night. To think how abrupt she'd been with David in the beginning and now he only had to look at her and she felt like she was melting. 'I love you, David,' she sang out loud, 'love you, love you, love you.'

The phone rang at the side of her bed. As expected it was Jan. She told her about her experience earlier that day when Lauren had worked out who she was. 'My problem is,' she finished, 'I think everyone is a reporter looking for me.'

'I have a confession, Kelly,' Jan said. 'Sean has found out that you've gone to Tunisia and he knows when you are due back. I'd made a note of it by the telephone. I know it was stupid but I didn't think. Sean's been on and on at me to tell him but I didn't. When he found my note by the phone and the brochure on Tunisia on the lower shelf of the coffee table he worked it all out. We had a flaming row and I finished with him.'

'I'm sorry.'

'Don't be, it would have happened sooner or later anyway. I'm just worried that the paparazzi will be waiting for you when you get home. You could always wear that black wig.'

'Maybe I will. Or maybe I'll just give them an interview and tell them I've been on holiday, no drama.'

'Everything all right with David? Will he be with you?'

'I doubt it. I still haven't told him the truth. I should have confided in him in the beginning but I was worried when I found out his brother is a reporter. I tried to tell him today but the words wouldn't come, not when he was being so affectionate. I didn't want to spoil the moment. He's talking about us coming back to Tunisia.'

Jan laughed. 'You'd better tell him before you get on the plane home or he'll be in for a terrible shock if all the reporters are there to greet you.'

* * *

She went down early for dinner and found the other three in the bar.

'Join me in an orange juice,' Sally smiled.

'Sally and Leo have some news for you,' David said.

'We're having a baby,' Leo announced proudly.

'That's brilliant!'

'It wasn't part of our plan I must admit, but sometimes the best things happen when you don't plan them.'

'How far are you?' David wanted to know.

'Two days,' Leo grinned.

'Can you tell that quickly?' David was amazed.

'I can,' Sally said. 'I'm never late. I didn't think Leo would be pleased but once he got over the shock he was thrilled, weren't you darling?'

'Absolutely!'

'I think that's wonderful,' David said. 'I don't think men think about babies like girls but once you meet the right one it's different.'

'And have you met the right one?' Leo teased.

'I think so.' David's eyes met hers and held.

Just imagine being married to David, waking up every morning and finding him there, bearing his children. Could it ever happen?

A wave of sadness engulfed her. Maybe she was worrying unnecessarily. Sally hadn't expected the kind of reception she'd had from Leo when she gave him the news. But that was different. Sally had told her that on occasions she had forgotten to take her pill but that wasn't like telling one lie after another to the person you supposedly loved.

Leo wasn't too keen to go to Hammamet as they'd been there previously but David said they'd go anyway.

'Don't get lost, Kelly,' Sally laughed, 'like you did in Sousse.'

'Don't worry,' David replied, 'I'll hold on tightly to her.'

A whole wonderful day to spend alone with David. No, she couldn't risk telling him this evening. Tomorrow, she promised herself, I'll find a way. Jan was right; he'd need to know before they arrived back in Bristol.

She pushed it to the back of her mind that evening as they sat laughing and chatting. When they danced David held her so close that their bodies felt like they had melted together.

'Tomorrow will be our last evening,' Sally greeted her as they went back to the table.

I know what Cinderella must have felt like, Kelly thought.

6

They set off immediately after breakfast for a visit to Hammamet. David had hired a taxi for the day and he sat in the back of the car with her, his arm around her shoulders.

'When I first met you,' he murmured, 'I thought you were really gorgeous but very stuck up.'

'And now?'

'I just think you're gorgeous and I'm glad I persevered. The longer I know you, the more gorgeous you get.'

'A week isn't very long to get to know anyone,' she warned, thinking how quickly he could change his mind.

'I like to think I'm pretty good at weighing people up. You had me fooled in the beginning and I couldn't make you out but now I feel I know you so well. You're sweet, you're beautiful but you don't trade on it. I guess you're absolutely perfect.'

Kelly wriggled uncomfortably and David mistook her worrying as modesty. He kissed the top of her head. 'I'm embarrassing you now but I meant every word.'

Their taxi driver had switched on his radio and to the strains of Tunisian melodies she asked, 'What do you think of people who tell lies?'

'Now where did that question come from? Believe me, I'm not lying when I tell you I think you're wonderful. Has someone been telling you lies then? Look over there, a shepherd with his sheep. It's like going back into the past, into biblical times. It's only when you get into the heart of the countryside that you get a glimpse of how it used to be.'

Another chance missed to tell him that she was the liar. Here in the taxi was hardly the place to disillusion him. There wasn't a right place or a right time. Perhaps when she explained the circumstances he would understand her

94

predicament. She'd hold on to that possibility.

The taxi agreed to give them a couple of hours to wander around before taking them on to Jasmine Hammamet.

'I love the beach,' Kelly said, 'especially when it's like this with pale soft sand and an inviting blue sea. We should have brought our swimming costumes and towels.'

'We won't be here that long, just a taster in case you chose to come here for our honeymoon, like Sally and Leo.'

He felt her stiffen. 'Am I presuming too much, Kelly?'

'You are rushing things. I do love you, David, but like I've told you lots of times, you don't really know me.'

'I know you well enough to know I want you to marry me. In case you think otherwise, I don't make a habit of proposing to girls. In fact I've never done it before.' He smiled. 'Come to think of it, I'm not sure you've said yes. So I'll ask you again. Will you marry me?'

'David, ask me again on the plane home. If you still want to marry me, the answer is yes.'

'What's so special about the plane?'

'It's not the plane, it's by then I'll have plucked up courage to tell you the truth, the whole truth.'

He was not taking her too seriously. 'You're still intent on being my lady of mystery. Are you the daughter of a murderer, were you left as a baby abandoned in a hospital toilet, were you had up for shoplifting when you were a child?'

'You're making a joke of it,' she said tightly.

'Because it doesn't matter. The past is the past. I've told you before I can't see that it can be that bad.'

He was so far away from the true situation.

He led her into one of the hotels off the beach and he had a boukha, a local drink, and coke. 'It's a bit like white rum. Want to try it in place of your orange juice? I know you're not

96

pregnant.' He pretended to look worried. 'You're not, are you?'

'Yes, all right, I'll try it, and no I am most definitely not pregnant!'

He clinked her glass. 'Here's to our future!'

After a visit to the medina where Kelly refused to let David buy her a necklace, they bought a pack of dates and some small biscuits dripping with honey, an unconventional lunch.

'I'm buying a pack of spices. In fact I'm buying two, one for my mother and one for you when you cook me some wonderful meals.'

'I've not had much experience of cooking,' Kelly admitted.

'Wait until I tell my mother I'm going to marry the most amazing girl in the world even if she can't cook! She'll like you, Kelly, I know she will. She can't wait for me and my brother Simon to get married.'

Simon the reporter. If Jan was right, and she could expect the paparazzi to be waiting for her when she arrived in

Bristol, could Simon be there?

They met up with the taxi and were taken to Jasmine Hammamet just a few miles away. It was like Port el Kantaoui, a man-made port but more spread out and it hadn't been there long enough to develop an atmosphere. The shop owners still came and tried to entice you into their premises but if you didn't know differently you could have thought you were in Spain with the wide promenades and walkways.

Next they went to Nabuel. Kelly was impressed with the distinctively charming town with centuries of old tradition of ceramics and pottery. She loved the intricate designs as exquisite as fine paintings.

'If you won't let me buy you anything,' David complained, 'what about a little phial of perfume? It's produced here. They particularly go in for orange and jasmine. In the end she accepted a small bottle of jasmine perfume.

'It's our very last evening,' she

pointed out on their way home, 'and I promise I'll tell you the truth somehow later today.'

She snuggled against him wishing it could all be very different.

* * *

Sally was in high spirits as they ate their evening meal. She was so thrilled about the baby and already wondering if it would be a boy or a girl and talking about names. 'What someone's called alters their whole personality, don't you think?' she asked Kelly.

'Perhaps.' Was Jasmine different from Kelly although they were one and the same?

'It's karaoke tonight,' Sally reminded her. 'I promise I won't railroad you into singing though.'

Their very last evening and a way to tell David the truth. She would sing one of Jasmine James's songs and he would know.

As the karaoke machine was set up

Kelly felt more nervous than at any of the auditions her mother had taken her to before she was famous. She knew what she would sing. It was her first big hit and the words could have been written for the occasion.

'I'm going to sing tonight,' she announced.

'You don't need to,' Sally frowned, 'you really don't. You don't need to prove anything to anyone.'

'I want to sing.' It was stretching the truth but it had to be done.

'You look terrified.'

'In that case I'll have a boukha and coke to give me courage. I tried it while we were out and I think I could develop a taste for it.'

She went over to the DJ to put her name down to sing and she told him what song she had chosen.

'That's a great number,' he said. 'It's a difficult song to sing though, not many can hit the top notes.'

She smiled at him. 'Are you trying to put me off?'

'Not at all. I'm just pointing out that you require quite a range in your voice for that particular song in case you'd prefer to sing something else.'

'No, it has to be that song.'

'Jasmine James is a favourite of mine. Come to think of it, you look a bit like her. I suppose you've been told that before.'

She returned to their table and David said, 'Are you sure about singing, Kelly? You were so adamant that you didn't want to last time.'

She took a gulp of her drink. 'I'm absolutely sure.'

'I don't think I'll sing this time,' Sally said.

'That sounds like a good idea,' Leo grinned.

It was the usual karaoke, a couple of them were quite good and the others just believed they were. Kelly supposed that was what made it such good entertainment.

And then suddenly it was her turn.

From the very first kiss I knew you

were for me. How could our love be wrong? You are my destiny . . .

The song went on to say that whatever the future held, whoever thought their love couldn't last, they knew differently.

The applause at the end of the song was deafening and there were shouts of 'More!' coming from the enthusiastic holidaymakers.

'Wow!' Sally exclaimed when she returned to the table. She could see that Sally had worked out the truth of the situation as she whispered, 'You really are, aren't you?'

She nodded briefly before turning to David. 'Those words were for you.'

'Thank you,' he returned, smiling, 'but no one will stand in our way. You actually have an amazing voice, you know.'

★ ★ ★

So he still had no idea who she was. To David she was still Kelly who just happened to have a good singing voice. Lots of the holidaymakers came over to say they thought she was brilliant.

Later when they went up to their rooms Kelly said, 'Do you think we could talk?' and followed him into his room.

David wrapped his arms around her waist. 'We could, but I've a much better idea.'

'I'm serious.' She turned her face from his kiss so his lips touched her hair. 'I need to explain. I know I should have told you earlier but . . . '

'And I've told you it didn't matter, Kelly, and that I love you. Have you robbed a bank?'

'Don't try and make it into a joke. I've a feeling that when I've told you, you won't actually find it funny.'

He took his arms away from her. 'Right then my mystery lady, put me out of my misery and reveal all.'

They were both sitting on his bed and he was waiting for her to speak. Her throat felt hot and tight now the moment had arrived. She tried to believe it would be all right, that he would find it somehow amusing even, and if he wasn't too pleased then he would understand. Sally had been worried about telling Leo about the baby she reminded herself, and that had worked out just fine.

'David, let me say at the beginning that I'm sorry. I didn't want to deceive you but once you tell a lie it leads to another and another and . . .'

'And another?' he teased, smiling at her.

She tried again. 'When I first came on this holiday wearing a black wig it was because I was scared of being recognised. I wanted time to myself to think my life through. I wasn't looking for further complications and I most definitely didn't expect to fall in love. Being with you was so fantastic I didn't want it to end.'

'And has it ended?' The smile had gone from his face and was replaced with a frown of confusion. 'What are you saying; that it was fun while it lasted, but now the holiday is over?'

'What I'm saying is I'm Jasmine James.'

He groaned. 'You really are, aren't you? Tonight when you sang I did wonder and then I told myself you couldn't be. I didn't want you to be. Why? Why did you have to make out you were someone else? Why did you let me believe we had something going for us when all the time you were amusing yourself letting me think we had a future?'

'We still could have,' she whispered.

He burst out laughing. 'Don't be silly!'

'I chose that song because the words seemed to say what I'm trying to say and making such a mess of.'

'There is no future for us, Kelly, or should I call you Jasmine? You and I live in different worlds.' He moved from the bed and began pacing restlessly up and down the room. 'Where is my sweet little girl with no money and some problem that I thought was small enough for me to sort out for her? You must have been having a good laugh to yourself all the while. I don't follow the gossip columns but even I know who Jasmine James is. She's always dating some guy or other, beautiful, sexy, sure of herself. She is nothing like my Kelly!'

'My agent fixed up the dates for photo shoots. I went along with it because I've been brainwashed since the age of twelve to do what was expected of me, that he knew best. There's never been a big romance in my life, there really hasn't. In the end I couldn't take it any more, it was like I couldn't breathe properly. And the worst part of it was that I was supposed to be grateful because I had what so many girls strived for. If I hadn't come away I think I would have been heading for a nervous breakdown.'

'And now?'

'Now I can see clearly.'

'In that case,' he said coldly, 'I'm glad

I was of some help.'

'I love you, David,' Kelly pleaded.

'Not enough to trust me. I don't think you love me, Kelly. You've been playing a part, needing a break from being a celebrity, seeing if you could carry it off. To sum it up, you've been having a laugh. You let me make a complete fool of myself for your own amusement with no remorse.'

'It wasn't like that at all. I wanted to tell you the truth but I didn't dare when I knew your brother was a reporter . . . '

There was no mirth in his laugh this time, it was harsh and bitter. 'How self-centred you are, Kelly! My brother would hardly be interested in your false life. He's a war correspondent!'

'You didn't tell me that.'

'I didn't intentionally keep any information from you. I can't say the same about you.'

'I still love you, David,' she whispered.

'Don't play any more games, Kelly. Like I said, we live in different worlds.

How come you were so short of money?'

'That was the truth; I did leave my cards behind. If you give me your address, I'll pay you back any money you've spent on me.'

'Keep your money! That's not important.'

'Don't you love me, not even the tiniest bit?' she begged.

'How can I? I don't even know who you are!'

'So this is goodbye?'

'You know it has to be, it could never work between us. I'm trying to understand why you couldn't tell me the truth in the beginning.'

She blinked away the tears. 'Maybe it was because I dreaded you'd react as you are doing now.'

'It was wonderful while it lasted. I'll follow your career with great interest, perhaps one day I'll tell my kids 'I knew Jasmine James'.'

'It doesn't have to be like that, David. You could tell them 'I met your mummy on holiday in Tunisia and we fell deeply and madly in love'.'

'This isn't one of those romantic songs you sing; this is real life, Kelly! You're already married to fame, to the limelight. You might have wanted to escape from it briefly, and I'm flattered that I was part of the fantasy, but you've different expectations of life and I'm not kidding myself that I could ever satisfy them.'

'I'm not going to humiliate myself any longer so I'll say goodnight.' She walked out of the room with as much dignity as she could manage.

★ ★ ★

David shut his bedroom door. This was the last thing he'd expected. He'd thought he was such a good judge of character, that he knew and understood Kelly so well, that he adored her and wanted to spend the rest of his life caring for her. Since he'd met her he had been mentally making plans. His flat was very much a bachelor pad, hardly suitable for starting married life. He'd put it on the market and they'd look for somewhere else. A small house with a garden perhaps. Perhaps they could even have a family too, like Leo and Sally. Yes, his imagination had taken him that far. Since he'd met her his whole attitude to life had changed and he'd wanted with Kelly what he'd found himself avoiding with every other girl he'd dated. It had been as though all his life he'd been waiting just for her.

Well, he'd simply have to get over her. In future he wouldn't let his heart rule his head. Maybe one day he'd laugh about his holiday romance that was just that — but he didn't truly think he would ever find it funny. His one time he'd actually been ready for commitment, would have welcomed it. What had she done to him?

* * *

It had been worse that she'd thought. It was over. As final as that. David had been so angry, so unforgiving. She knew he felt mortified by her deceit but surely he could have tried to see it from her point of view, to have somehow forgiven her, if not completely. They could surely have worked something out. If necessary she would have given up her career. He hadn't given her time to say that.

They'd said their goodbyes in the coldest, saddest way she could imagine. Whoever said it was better to have loved and lost than never to have loved at all didn't know what they were talking about. She didn't ever want to feel like this again, so alone, so wretched. He said he didn't know her but did she really know him? Where was the kind, compassionate man she'd believed him to be? He'd all but ordered her out of his room and if he'd shown any feeling towards her then it was one of contempt.

Stop crying Kelly, she thought to herself miserably. Tomorrow she could well have the paparazzi to contend with. Well, she'd cope with that, she wouldn't bother to wear the black wig. And she'd smile for the cameras. No one would know her heart felt like it was breaking.

7

Not being able to sleep, Kelly had done her packing last night so after her morning shower it was simply a matter of adding the last few items to her case. When she went down for breakfast David was already there but there was no sign of Sally and Leo. She brought her coffee and yoghurt over and sat down facing him. He didn't look like he'd slept well either.

'Is it all right if I sit here, David?'

'It's not up to me where you sit.'

'If you'd rather, I could move to another table.'

'It's not a problem.' A long pause. 'Perhaps I overreacted last night but what you told me took me completely by surprise.'

There was a sudden surge of hope. 'You had a right to be angry, I know that. My only defence is that I never intended to hurt you and . . . ' She wanted to say, 'and I still love you,' but couldn't trust his response.

'No point in going over and over it. Sally and Leo will be here any time now. We can at least act civil to each other, not make it uncomfortable for them. In fact I can see them coming now.'

'Hi!' Kelly managed as Sally and Leo sat down.

'Hi!' Sally gulped.

'Sally . . . ' Kelly's own unhappiness was put on hold as she looked at her friend's face. Sally's eyes were red and swollen with crying.

'Whatever's wrong?'

'It was a false alarm,' Leo told them quietly. 'No baby.'

'I was so sure,' Sally mumbled. 'Now I feel like a real idiot.'

'No, of course you're not,' Kelly told her gently. 'I know how upset you are but it will happen, this baby. Hold on to that.'

'When we go home, Kelly, you will

keep in touch, won't you?'

'I promise. And I'll introduce you to my friend, Jan.' Her mouth trembled into a smile. 'If you still want your hair cut, Jan will do it for you, my treat. Just imagine what it would have been like if I'd done it for you!'

'No, I think you were right. Leo likes my hair long.'

'You're beautiful however you wear your hair, Sally,' Leo told her gently.

'Next time I'll make sure I really am pregnant before I go blabbing.'

'I'll start saving up for an enormous teddy,' David said. 'Leo has my phone number so let me know as soon as you get the good news.'

It was a sombre last day and although David was civil there was no warmth in him and he didn't choose to sit by her on the coach ride to the airport. She would have liked to have left on better terms but it wasn't to be.

A lady travelling on her own sat next to her telling her how much she'd enjoyed the karaoke and what a delightful voice she had.

Sally and Leo could sense the tension between Kelly and David despite David's politeness. It was the politeness of strangers.

Her time at the airport dragged by as they waited for their plane. Yesterday they'd been so happy but now it had all changed.

David and Leo had gone for a walk around the 'duty free' and she and Sally sat with the hand luggage.

'Will you see David when you go home?' Sally asked

'He doesn't want anything to do with me.' The tears still threatened and Kelly blinked them away. 'I admit I did tell lies but I was here in disguise and didn't want people to know. I wanted to be Kelly — plain Kelly. David didn't even try and see it from my point of view.'

'He was in shock. He still looks longingly at you when he thinks no one is looking,' Sally attempted to reassure her.

'I hardly think so! Don't worry, I'll get over him somehow. After all, a week ago we hadn't even met.'

If she was going to survive, if she had to be confident enough to do battle with Todd, then she had to be tough.

★　★　★

On the plane Kelly occupied the aisle seat next to Sally and Leo sat by the window seat on the other side.

'Are you all right, Kelly?'

Kelly squeezed her friend's hand reassuringly. 'Sure. What about you?'

'I'm all right, disappointed I suppose but at least I now know what I want. I can't believe I didn't even realise how much I wanted a baby. I thought David might have tried harder to sit by you.'

'I did too,' Kelly agreed, 'but I can appreciate how he feels.'

'Could be he's trying not to give into his feelings, this macho thing.'

'We were so close,' Kelly sighed, 'and now we're like strangers. If we'd sat together then it could well have been that neither of us would have known what to say. How many times can you say 'I'm sorry'?'

'I think he's being very stubborn!'

'I'm going to have to learn to forget him.'

'He does love you. That's why it hurts so much.'

At that moment David walked down the aisle. 'Can we talk, Kelly? There's a spare seat next to me.'

Her heart started to race as she remembered she'd told him that if he wanted to marry her to ask her again on the plane. Is that what he intended?

'Excuse me,' she said to both Sally and Leo.

She sat down next to David. 'What is it?' she enquired, keeping her voice as even as she could.

'You and me,' he said quietly. 'I don't want us to finish on bad terms.'

She could hardly breathe. 'Me neither.'

'I'm trying to see it from your angle.

I made demands on you that were ridiculous. It was like I was bewitched. I guess I'm trying to make excuses for my arrogance.'

'I didn't think you were arrogant. You had every right to be annoyed.'

'No, I didn't.'

'Is that it?'

'More or less. I can't pretend I won't miss you but . . . '

'But you wouldn't want to marry me?'

'It was a nice dream while it lasted.'

She didn't pursue the subject, didn't let him tell her again why it would never work.

'So what will you do now?'

'I've been thinking about that. I've a friend who has an architect's office in London. He's been trying to interest me in going into partnership with him. Jake's an old friend, we met at Uni. I think I'll take him up on the offer.'

If she'd had any hope at all she felt it evaporating.

'It will mean selling my flat in Bristol

and moving to London. It will be a fresh start but I'll welcome that. Do you want to stay in touch?'

'No point is there,' she said with as much pride as she could muster. 'I expect I'll hear how you are doing from Sally. I hope it all works out for you.'

'You too,' he said sadly. 'Sorry I was so harsh last night. Now I've calmed down I can see you had your reasons for how you acted. I hope life works out for you too, Kelly, I really do.'

She felt emotionally drained as she walked back to her seat. She didn't cry, she'd used up all her tears.

When they arrived at Bristol David was there lifting her luggage from the crowded carousel. 'Kelly . . . '

'Thank you but I could have managed. Good luck in your future venture.'

Her case was one of the first to arrive. She waved goodbye to the others and made her way through customs and then outside where Jan was waiting to meet her.

'Your dad's here with the car. Let's make a dash for it.'

Jan was right about the paparazzi. She hoped she wouldn't be recognised but it was not to be.

'You've had your hair cut, Jasmine, but it suits you.' There were a series of flashes of photography.

'Okay.' She brought a smile from somewhere. 'A very quick interview.'

'You didn't tell your mother where you were going. Was that deliberate?'

'You could say it was thoughtless but when I realised she was worried about me I got word to her. I've had a great holiday but there must be much more interesting people around to write about.'

'Everyone's interested in you, Jasmine,' a woman reporter put in. 'Tomorrow the salons will be full of girls wanting their hair cut in your style.'

A few more questions and they let her go. It hadn't been so bad after all. And she'd coped without Todd there orchestrating the event.

'I'm going to drive you to Jan's, Angel,' her father, Bob, advised, as thankfully she and Jan reached his car. 'Then we'll ring your mum.'

★ ★ ★

David watched with horror as the paparazzi swarmed around Kelly throwing question after question at her.

He had the urge to go over to assist her but it would only have complicated things. As it was she was conducting herself with a mature confidence that he hadn't known she possessed.

As if reading his thoughts Leo said, 'You couldn't get near her anyway, David. She's certainly handling herself as though it happens all the time — which I suppose it does.'

'Yeah, the downside to being famous. The more I think about it the more I can see why she was so secretive as to who she was.'

Sally and Leo were being picked up

by neighbours and David had his car parked at the airport. He threw his case in the boot and slammed it shut.

As soon as he got home he'd let Jake know he'd like to be his partner in London. Next he'd ring a couple of estate agents and ask them to come round to view his property and decide on one to market his flat.

He was about to start a new chapter in his life. There'd be plenty to think about which was good.

More than anything he needed to keep his mind off Kelly.

★ ★ ★

Bob stayed a while at Jan's and had a cup of tea with them. He left with a reminder to her to ring her mother.

'I promise I'll ring her the moment you go. Thanks for everything.'

Once they were on their own Jan wanted to hear every detail of her holiday in Tunisia. 'Is it really over between you and David?'

'I can answer that in one word. Yes.'

Kelly fished out her old mobile phone from her bundle of possessions Jan had kept for her and rang her mother.

Zara's first words to her were, 'I've been worried sick!' There was a dramatic pause. 'Whatever possessed you — '

The phone must have been taken from her mother by Todd. 'It's all right Kelly, you're home now. So when do we see you again?'

'I'll stay at Jan's tonight and drive home tomorrow — if that's all right.'

'Of course, sweetie. We've lots to talk about.'

'Yes, we have Todd,' Kelly said firmly.

Jan was surprised. 'You sounded very assertive. It might only have been a week but you're different somehow.'

'I have to learn to toughen up, Jan. Otherwise I think I'll go to pieces and I don't intend to let myself do that. If I'm honest, I am upset about David; I fell for him in a big way. However I'm not going to mope around. You simply can't have everything you want in life, can you?'

* * *

After breakfast next morning she drove home. She pressed the special hand control she kept concealed in the car which allowed the gates to her home to open so she could enter. The house was a present to her mother but Kelly still lived there. The gardener waved to her from the sit-on tractor as he cut the wide lawns. The house and grounds were her mother's pride and joy. Yes, her mother had devoted herself to her success and deserved the house; she'd been the driving ambition. I'm very lucky Kelly told herself, but she didn't feel lucky. David was out of her life and it hurt so much.

Both Zara and Todd were waiting for her. Any moment now and Todd would explode. She was ready for him.

'Have you had breakfast, Kelly?' Zara asked.

'Yes, thank you.'

'Good holiday?' Todd enquired spooning sugar into his coffee.

Kelly took the cup of coffee her mother was offering. 'Thank you. Was that meant as sarcasm, Todd?'

He surprised her by saying, 'No, it wasn't. You were right — you have been working too hard.'

It occurred to her for the first time that she held all the trump cards. 'I don't know why it suddenly happened but it all got on top of me. I know how you feel about publicity, Todd, but from now on I want to try and be me. Perhaps I'm not as exciting as the fabrication that was Jasmine, in fact I know I'm not, but the problem is I don't even want to be. I'm not going to be part of any publicity stunts in the future.'

'But you still want to sing?'

'I love to sing, you know that.'

'I'm sorry if I always pushed you too

hard,' Zara said softly. 'You have a beautiful singing voice, much better than I ever had. I want you to be successful but I also want you to be happy. Both Todd and I agree that in future you must have more of a say.'

Kelly laughed. 'I thought I was in for one hell of an argument. I know you've always wanted the best for me, Mum. It's been my fault for not telling you how I really feel. I think I've only just worked it out myself.'

'There's that charity event next week,' Todd reminded her. 'Do you still want to do it?'

'Of course I do! What I don't want to do is never have a day to call my own. I seem to be either working or travelling somewhere. I'm sorry if that sounds ungrateful after all your efforts, Todd.'

'You make a lot of sense, sweetie. I don't want you to burn yourself out.'

'I was all ready for a battle, so thanks for being so understanding.'

'How would you feel about doing something different, Kelly?'

127

'Different, Todd? Like what?'

'Being in a London show.'

Now she was intrigued. 'Singing?'

He smiled. 'Singing, dancing, acting . . . '

'Where did this come from?'

'I've had a phone call from Desmond Drake. He's working on a new production of *Smiling Through Tears* and both he and the writer have suggested you as the perfect leading lady. It would mean a hell of a lot of hard work so you might not be up for it the way you are feeling at the moment, but I have to say it's a big compliment. It's expected to be a smash hit. What do you think?'

'I don't know what to think. I know I have a good singing voice, I've had dancing tuition along the way but acting . . . '

'There will be a coach but it would mean giving yourself up to it completely. And once the show opens you're talking about having the stamina for eight shows a week.'

'On the plus side,' Kelly said

thoughtfully, 'it would mean living in one place, putting-down roots even though they might be new ones. Can we meet the producer and discuss the possibility? I'm not sure if my acting would be good enough.'

So much for taking things easily! It was just what she needed though, a new challenge; no time to feel life had dealt her a raw deal because she couldn't have David.

8

Since the holiday, she and Sally phoned each other at regular intervals as did Leo and David. It wasn't as easy to forget David as she had hoped.

'David always asks if we've heard from you and how you are. And, guess what, he's left Bristol and gone into partnership with a friend in London so you could literally bump into him one day.'

'I shouldn't think so. London's a large place.'

'I could give you his phone number,' Sally suggested.

'No, don't do that. I need to keep focused. Desmond Drake was eager for me to join the company initially but that doesn't stop him from getting at me at times. I thought Todd was tough but he was a pussy cat in comparison with Des.'

'So why don't you pack it in?'

'I need the challenge and I need to not let him down. We open in a couple of weeks and I sincerely hope he doesn't decide to substitute my under-study at the very last moment. She's eager and experienced.'

'Are you happy?'

'I've tried happiness and it doesn't last,' she said with a tinge of cynicism. 'I'm certainly more settled. I've rented an apartment and I'm enjoying living on my own, looking after myself for the first time. The last six weeks have flown by. I've loads to achieve before the opening night and sometimes it seems an impossible task. Every day I wonder if it is going to be my last.'

Sally changed the subject. 'How about if I give David your telephone number instead?'

'Has he asked for it?'

'No, but . . . '

'Then don't,' Kelly said decisively.

Kelly was always pleased to hear from Sally but for once she felt uneasy and disturbed after her call. But she had to stay focussed. It was important she gave all her commitment to the show. She'd been warned the critics could be scathing when the show opened. They simply couldn't afford it to be a flop.

In some ways she knew that casting her as the leading lady was a gamble and the stakes were very high. It was like belonging to one big extended family; she loved the theatre environment but there were many occasions when, like any family, tempers could be frayed and disagreements occured.

She just hoped tomorrow would be better.

★   ★   ★

The musical was based on a book about four orphaned children who became split up when their mother died. She was playing the part of the oldest, married to a man twenty years her senior so she could have her younger sister and two brothers to live with her.

'Let's see some raw emotion Jasmine!' Des had roared at her. 'You've married a man you don't really love so you can make a home for your siblings. It's not working out, however; the boys are in bad company heading for trouble, your sister is flighty and looking for fun and your husband isn't as long suffering as you'd thought he'd be. He's disillusioned with you as a wife and he makes no bones about it. No one seems to care how you feel. Make me care, Jasmine, make the audience care, lose your inhibitions and feel the part. Think of the worst moment of your life and divert it into this part and let the emotion engulf you.'

Her mind went back to David that last night in Tunisia and she relived the hurt, the disappointment, the humiliation.

Her eyes brimmed with the tears she'd held in check since she'd moved to London. She'd been determined she would get over David and the only way was to shut her feelings away. It hadn't been easy and she wasn't sure it was working but she'd learnt to keep a cap on her emotions. Now Desmond was trying to break down the barriers, giving her permission to give way to the still raw heartache she was experiencing. She directed the pain, the loss, the hopelessness of her situation into the part she was playing. She felt drained and liberated at the same time.

'Jasmine, I'd like you to stay behind at the end of rehearsals,' Desmond ordered loudly.

So, it still wasn't good enough. Would he tell her it wasn't working out and it would be better if she left the show now?

When they were alone he said, 'I'd like to go through that scene again.'

Her confidence plummeted. 'Wasn't it any good?'

'It wasn't good, Jasmine.' He gave her one of his rare smiles. 'It was brilliant! I just want to know you can do it again, that I didn't imagine the pathos you portrayed.'

It was the first real praise she'd had from him.

Her voice echoed through the empty auditorium and at the end Des clapped enthusiastically.

'Right, get your coat Jasmine! What a breakthrough! I'm going to take you for a slap up meal to celebrate.'

He took it for granted that she would want to go with him. Des, recently divorced, was a powerful man, undoubtedly good looking with his dark hair and dark, almost black eyes. She was amazed at his sudden interest in her but it could be no more than professional. She hoped so. She admired him wholeheartedly but the last thing she needed was any personal involvement.

'You're a very private person, Jasmine,' he commented between mouthfuls of fillet steak.

'I try to be but it's not easy when you're in the public eye.'

'I don't count what the newspapers say,' he dismissed. 'I just feel that inside you is a secret little box labelled 'passion' and I'd like to be the one to open it.'

His dark, brooding eyes forced her to look at him.

She blushed under their scrutiny. 'You're making me sound more exciting than I really am. I have to be straight with you, Des. At the moment all I want to do is lose myself in the part I'm playing, to be worthy of the opportunity. The one thing I don't want is involvement with anyone.'

'At the moment you said.' He shrugged. 'It will be all the better for the waiting. Come on, I'll take you home. We have a busy schedule tomorrow.'

He left her in the foyer of her apartment block; a quick peck on the cheek and he was gone. He hadn't put her through the embarrassment of not inviting him in. He was right — they had a busy day tomorrow. He'd been very pleasant but she guessed he wasn't used to being rebuffed and he wasn't going to go out of his way to make her life easy. If she was ever to get another word of praise from him she'd have to more than deserve it.

She closed the door to her apartment and went into the kitchen and switched on the kettle. Des had kept filling up her wine glass and she thought a cup of coffee would clear her head. Desmond Drake was a very attractive man she acknowledged and she wished she could feel something for him but she couldn't. It was nearly three months since she'd returned from Tunisia and she should be over David now. He'd come so briefly into her life but she missed him so much. She'd love to see him again if only for a few minutes. He was in London, that much she knew, but where?

It wasn't all that late, not too late to ring Sally for a chat.

'Hi, Kelly! Lovely to hear from you. I did try ringing you earlier but your mobile was switched off.'

'Des goes mad if anyone's phone rings.'

'He sounds like a monster.'

'It's just his way. He is giving the production total dedication and expects the same from everyone else. He's been particularly hard on me but today I received my first ever compliment from him. I've only just left him; he took me out for a meal.'

'So David is in the past?' Sally probed.

'I wish I could say yes to that,' Kelly sighed.

'The whole situation is plain stupid,' Sally told her. 'He's so interested in what you're doing, he always asks. Sometimes I think he only rings so he can keep up to date with what's happening in your life.'

'He was the one to make the break,' Kelly reminded her.

'He was in shock,' Sally defended him. 'Now he's too stubborn to go chasing after you; not only stubborn, he probably thinks there is no chance now you're going to be an even bigger star. You'll have to tell him how you feel, Kelly.'

'I'm not setting myself up for another dose of humiliation.'

'You're both daft.'

'I have to give all my attention to the show,' Kelly protested. 'Anyway, enough about me; how are you?'

'I'm pregnant!'

'That's terrific!'

'This time it is definite. I've been checked out by the doctor. Leo's been treating me like I'm made of fine porcelain. The other thing I keep forgetting to mention is that I've been in touch with your friend, Jan. She comes and does my hair — Leo's too. We've become quite close. When your show opens we're all coming to see it. Oh, that was meant to be a secret but I'm useless at keeping secrets, so you'll have to pretend you didn't know.'

'I'll look forward to seeing you then.'

'Jan's bringing David's mum with her.'

'David's mum?' Kelly repeated in amazement. 'How would she know David's mum?'

'Hasn't she told you? David introduced them. David was here one of the days when Jan was here doing my hair and she cut his. They've been in touch ever since.'

'Right. I'd better go, Sally. I've got a heavy day tomorrow so I need to get my sleep.'

This was one thing she hadn't expected. David and Jan. Well, they were both free agents so why not? *Stop it,* she thought to herself, *you've absolutely no right to be jealous.* Right or not she was fiercely jealous. Not only that, it gave a complete finality to her relationship with David.

Before she realised what she was doing she rang Jan. She didn't know quite what she was going to say but she had to speak to her.

She plunged right in. 'I was just speaking to Sally and she tells me you've met David.'

Jan showed no embarrassment. 'Yes, I have. I didn't tell you because I didn't know whether you wanted me to mention him in the circumstances. I was really mad with him for the way he treated you but once I'd met him I changed my mind. You're right, he really is dishy and so genuine, too.'

'Jan says you know his mother,' Kelly croaked, trying to stay calm.

'She's a really lovely lady, Kelly. With David now based in London and Simon working abroad so often, they asked me to keep an eye on her. I sometimes pop in for a cup of tea and a chat between hairdressing visits.'

She used the same excuse she'd used to Sally. 'I'd better go, got a heavy day tomorrow.'

'Fancy me knowing such a big star. I'm looking forward to coming to London for the show. Whoops, I think that was meant to be a secret but you would have guessed we'd want to come and see you. I hope you won't be too busy to see us.'

'No, of course not!'

'We'll always be friends, won't we Kelly?' Jan said fondly. 'I feel so proud of you.'

'Of course we'll always be friends.' *Even if you've stolen the man I love*, Kelly thought sadly, wiping away tears. She could cry if she wanted. Des told her not to hold her emotion in check, didn't he? All control gone she sobbed as though she would never be able to stop.

Next morning her eyes were still swollen from crying. She stayed in bed for a while with cotton wool pads on them that she'd soaked in ice cold water. It helped a little and the rest of the camouflage was achieved with clever make-up. With a final look in the mirror, she headed for the theatre.

There was a certain amount of tension in the cast that was overshadowed by the excitement.

Kelly hoped she wouldn't let them down. Supposing her acting wasn't good enough or she got out of step with the dance routine? *A career is all you have, so be grateful for it,* she thought. David belongs to Jan now; remember that and concentrate on what you have.

Later she went home to her empty apartment, switched on the kettle and made herself a cup of tea. She wondered what David was doing at that moment. How was she ever going to stop thinking about him?

Kelly jumped when her phone rang.

'Hi Kelly.'

'David?' she whispered.

'I've been talking to Sally. She said she thought you were worried about the opening of the show.'

A sympathy call? 'It's the first musical I've ever done but everyone's anxious. I'm told that's normal.'

'If you can find the time, perhaps we could meet up?' David asked.

She could see him again, reach out and touch him if only to shake his hand. 'Is that wise?' she sighed.

He laughed. 'What's wisdom got to do with anything? I suppose you must be busy though . . . '

Surely it wouldn't do any real harm to see him once again. She knew the score. He was with Jan but surely they could be friends?

'I am busy with rehearsals but if we could meet somewhere near the theatre we could go for a cup of coffee,' Kelly heard herself say.

'That would be great.' He sounded as tense as she was. 'Tomorrow?'

'I'd like that,' she answered breathlessly, honestly, naming the nearby coffee bar.

'I've been trying to pluck up courage to ring you but I suppose I thought you wouldn't want me to bother you.'

She was gripping the telephone receiver. 'So what changed your mind?'

'The need to see you again.'

'See you tomorrow then.'

She was holding on to the receiver long after he'd gone. He needed to see her again. Despite everything, all that he'd said that last night in Tunisia, he needed to see her again. Well, she knew about need, about longing. The song she'd sung that last night in Tunisia ran through her head.

Whatever was she thinking? David and Jan! She knew the score. Only David didn't know she knew of course. It could well be that Sally had hinted that she was grieving for him and he felt sorry for her and needed to tell her himself that he and Jan were now an item.

It would be awful. She might break down in tears even though she already knew about Jan. At the moment, with the worry of the show and in particular her own inadequacies, she could well make an embarrassing spectacle of herself. Why put herself through all that? The wise thing to do was to ring him back and cancel.

But she wouldn't; she wouldn't give up the chance to see him again, however brief, however painful.

What was it he'd said? She smiled as she recalled the words. What's wisdom go to do with anything?

9

She was glad of half an hour's break to meet David for coffee. Desmond had been in a foul mood all morning and she'd been the one to take the brunt of it.

Was she really so hopeless or was he paying her back for her cool reception when he'd taken her out? She didn't know. A couple of times she was close to walking out but she took the criticism and tried to do better, determined he was not going to break her will. If the show flopped it was not going to be because of her.

It wasn't far to the designated coffee bar but it hadn't been easy to get away and she was five minutes late. David was waiting for her and her heart stopped when she saw him. He looked so handsome in his smart navy suit and crisp white shirt. He stood up as she approached and kissed her cheek. Could you really faint from a friendly peck on the cheek she wondered?

Her voice had the funny breathless quality that he evoked. 'Sorry I'm a bit late, David.'

The waitress came over with her coffee that had obviously already been ordered. Kelly noted that his cup was empty.

'I was early,' he said as he saw her looking at it.

She smiled. 'In that case, even sorrier I'm late. It's not been a good morning as everyone's on edge with last minute nerves. I guess it's one of those days.'

She waited for what he had to say but he just smiled back.

Then, 'It's really great to see you again. Unfortunately, I can't stay long. I've got an unexpected appointment to meet a client. It could be a very big contract and we desperately need the work. It's not exactly a good time to be in architecture what with businesses nervous about expanding. If we get this job it will make all the difference to our future.'

Was he regretting meeting her? Was he making excuses so he didn't have to prolong the time he spent with her? Was he chickening out of telling her about his relationship with Jan?

'I hope it all goes well for you.'

He looked at his watch. 'I'm really sorry but I'm going to have to go. I did try to phone you but there was no reply on your mobile.'

'Desmond insists our phones are switched off when we're rehearsing.'

He was already standing up. 'Perhaps we could meet again? Go out for a meal sometime?'

'I'm very busy.'

He handed her his business card. 'I really am sorry about this. If you can fit me in . . . well, I'll leave it to you to ring me if you have any free time.'

He leaned over and planted another kiss on the top of her head. This time she didn't feel faint, just angry.

She was tired and emotionally

exhausted. She'd been dreading the opening of the show but now she'd be glad when it arrived. Then she'd know for certain whether she had made the grade or not. Todd's schedule had had her working non-stop and living out of a suitcase but he'd not treated her in the way Desmond did. He and her mother were due in London later that evening and she looked forward to Todd's reassurance. He'd always told her how good she was, had made her believe it.

Her mother, Zara, was moving into the apartment with her, and Todd would be staying at a hotel near the theatre. Kelly wondered what Desmond would have to say to Todd about her. Maybe he would tell Todd he had made a mistake in asking for her as she was useless.

'Oh, Mum, it's lovely to see you!' Kelly greeted her warmly, kissing her on both cheeks. 'I've had one hell of a day — it's good to see a friendly face.'

'Well, you have the apartment very

nice,' Zara said, 'and you're so organised. I don't know how you manage it all.'

'It hasn't been easy,' Kelly admitted, 'but I think it's been good for me. I'm so used to being looked after but now I'm in the real world. I'm tired though, and scared, very scared.'

'You'll be sensational,' Zara said.

Kelly laughed. 'You're my mother, you're biased. If you'd heard Desmond shouting the odds at me today you might think differently.'

'He's probably only trying to get the best out of you,' Zara told her

'Will something out of the freezer be all right, Mum? I haven't had much time for cooking.'

'How about a Chinese take-away?' Zara suggested. 'Then you can tell me all your news.'

'I can tell you that in a couple of sentences — or come to think of it, one sentence. I go to rehearsals, come home, tumble into bed and fall asleep. Sometimes I ask myself why I ever thought I could do it.'

'On second thoughts, let's break the mould and go out for a meal. We could go to Todd's hotel. I know he's looking forward to seeing you. Then in the morning I'll bring you breakfast in bed and tomorrow evening you can come home to a casserole.'

'Sounds good,' Kelly answered appreciatively. It was then her mobile phone rang.

It was Jan. 'Hi Kelly! I thought I'd give you a ring and see how you are coping with all the pressure of the show.'

'Scared and excited,' she replied. She wondered whether she should tell Jan she'd seen David earlier that day, but decided against it.

Jan had done nothing wrong and it would be spiteful of her to try and drive a wedge between them out of jealousy. It had been quite a day!

Even so, when David rang just as she and Zara were about to go out she was thrilled to hear from him.

'I know I said I'd leave it to you to ring but I wanted to speak to you so I couldn't wait that long. It was great to see you again, Kelly, and I'm sorry it was for such a short time. Is there any chance I could see you again soon?'

'How did your appointment go?' She needed time to think.

'It went well, seems we're the chosen architects for the job.'

'That's brilliant!'

'So can we celebrate the outcome?'

'Hold on.' She called over to Zara who was waiting by the door. 'Could you stretch the casserole tomorrow evening to three?'

'Of course,' Zara smiled. 'In fact I could invite Todd and make it four.'

'I'll give you my address, David. Come and join us for a meal tomorrow.'

With Zara and Todd there she couldn't betray Jan.

Zara was absolutely right. Todd was very pleased to see her. 'You look different, Kelly.'

She laughed. 'Do you mean tired and weary looking?'

'No, I mean more grown up, confident. Desmond thinks you are going to be just perfect in the part.'

'You must be joking!'

'What he actually said was there was a time when he wondered if you'd be strong enough for eight performances a week but now he feels you've shown that you will. It's a tough business, Kelly. What's impressed him is that you can take criticism and survive it.'

She shook her head. 'There were a couple of times today when I could have dissolved into tears.'

Todd looked at the wine list the waiter had put before him. 'The point is Kelly that you didn't. He was impressed and so am I. Will you trust me to choose the wine?'

She felt much happier when she and Zara left to go back to her apartment. And tomorrow evening she would see David again.

The opening night was getting very

near and now the excitement was stronger than the fear. Forget failure. She was going to show the public that she wasn't only a singer; she could dance and act too. She would put her heart and soul into the performance.

★　★　★

Todd and David arrived at her apartment within minutes of each other. David had brought wine and Todd had picked up a cheesecake, possibly at Zara's request.

Kelly set the table, excited that David was there, deciding that even if his interest now was in Jan she still wanted him for a friend.

She'd thought the evening could have been a little bit strained but it wasn't like that at all. David had now accepted she was in show business and wanted to hear all about what it was like to be part of a new production.

Zara was interested to learn that he was an architect. 'Just like Leonardo da

Vinci,' she complimented him.

'Hardly.' He grinned. 'I deal in industrial architecture — functional but not quite a work of art.'

'Art in its own way,' Zara insisted. 'Practical art.'

For once Kelly was even able to talk about her time in Tunisia and how it had been living in disguise. Looking back on it, the lies she'd had to tell didn't sound half as bad.

Zara laughed so much about Sally asking if Kelly could cut her hair that there were tears running down her face.

'You had no idea who Kelly was when you met,' Zara commented.

'Well, no, Zara. All the clues were there but I don't keep up with showbiz gossip. On the last night when Kelly sang at the karaoke I must have been the only fool there who didn't work it out immediately.'

He looked across at Kelly apologetically.

'I should have told you in the beginning, David, trusted you more,' she murmured softly.

Both Zara and Todd were looking at them speculatively.

If they had been on their own Kelly had a feeling that she would have been in David's arms and they would have implicitly forgiven each other.

Todd cleared his throat. 'I have an announcement to make.' He turned his attention on Kelly. 'I hope you won't mind, Kelly, but I've asked your mum if she'll marry me. She hasn't said a straightforward yes but we do love each other and I think she really wants your approval. We have known each other for years and . . .'

'And I think that's wonderful,' Kelly told him softly. She hugged him and then Zara. David offered his congratulations.

'I just happen to have a bottle of bubbly in the car!' Todd gushed happily. 'I'll go and get it.'

'It will only be a small wedding,' Zara told them when Todd went out to his car. 'You're invited of course, David.

Kelly's kept very quiet about you, I must say.'

'We're just good friends, Mum,' Kelly blushed.

'My goodness! You're talking like a showbiz star. I'm your mother don't forget. I should think you're more than good friends. Isn't that right, David?'

'Mum!'

David was saved from answering by the reappearance of Todd brandishing a bottle.

'You've had far too much drink to drive, Todd,' Zara said reprovingly. 'You'll have to leave your car here and get a taxi. I'll drive over to your hotel tomorrow with your car.'

'Just listen to her.' Todd grinned. 'She's nagging like a wife already.'

'I think I'll need to do the same,' David said, looking at his glass.

'You can share my taxi,' Todd offered. 'I suppose we'd better let Kelly get to bed so she's bright eyed and bushy tailed for tomorrow.'

Kelly smiled inwardly at the old

cliché. It explained exactly how she was feeling. David was going home in a taxi which meant that tomorrow there was a chance she would see him again when he came to collect his car the following day.

David didn't kiss her before he left but his eyes caressed her. *Sorry Jan,* she thought, *but I just love him so much.*

'Shall we have a cup of cocoa?' Kelly asked Zara when the men had left. 'It might help us sleep.'

Zara laughed, surprised. 'Don't you watch your calories any more?'

'Not so obsessively. I think I was letting myself get too thin. Also I get so much exercise with all the dancing we do at rehearsals that it keeps me slim. None of the dancers seem to have a weight problem. It has been hard work and sometimes Desmond can be unreasonable but he is such a perfectionist that we all forgive him. I've loved it all really.'

'I'm so proud of you, Kelly. I thought when you ran off to Tunisia without telling me that . . . '

'I'm sorry. I should have told you how I felt, trusted you. I didn't trust David either and that was the problem in the end.'

'You're very much in love with him, aren't you?'

Kelly poured hot milk over the cocoa powder in the mugs. 'Is it so obvious? He only has to look at me and I feel like I am dissolving. I can't see there will be much future for us though.'

'Why's that?'

'I'll be doing eight shows a week for quite a while to come — unless the show is a flop that is. He'll be working every day and I'll be working in the evenings. Not much of a relationship, is it?'

'You'll find a way to work it out. Others have. Love won't let you put obstacles in the way.'

Kelly stirred her cocoa.

'We spent a week together in Tunisia and then more or less agreed to go our separate ways. That doesn't sound very promising, does it?'

'What you can't deny is the feelings you have for each other. Don't be scared of them. Falling in love and having that love returned is one of the most wonderful experiences that can happen to you.'

'What a romantic you are, Mum.'

'All women are romantics,' Zara declared emphatically. 'The lucky ones can live out that dream.'

Kelly sighed. 'There is a problem.'

'Insurmountable?'

'David has met Jan — more than met her. It sounds as if she's practically part of the family. Jan goes and visits his Mum in Bristol quite often, gets on well with her. We've shared so much since we were both at primary school but we can't share David, can we? If we are both in love with him one of us is going to lose out and whatever the outcome we're hardly likely to stay best friends.'

'Are you saying you have to choose between Jan and David?'

'I might not even have that choice. I

don't know how David feels about Jan, what commitment they have made to each other. All I can think is how much I love him. I'm finding it very hard to look at this in anything but a selfish way.'

'One thing you've never been Kelly is selfish. For now concentrate on the show. Let life take its own course.'

Kelly nodded, suddenly feeling very tired. 'Goodnight, Mum, and thanks for the advice.'

As she undressed and slipped into bed she tried to blank her mind to encourage sleep but all she could think of was David.

10

David left Todd at his hotel. 'It's all right,' he insisted, 'I'll pay the taxi.' He gave the taxi driver his address which was in fact in the opposite direction, and thought what a wonderful evening it had been.

Zara and Todd had made him feel so welcome and as for Kelly . . . Seeing her again in London had been unbelievable.

She was even lovelier than he remembered her, so very sweet and caring as she enthused about Sally's pregnancy. That was what made her so special. There were lots of pretty girls around but Kelly's beauty was accentuated by the concern she showed for others. Being famous hadn't spoiled her. The way he'd spoken to her on their last evening in Tunisia, it was a wonder she wanted anything more to do with him. Yet she'd invited him over for dinner, introduced him to Zara and Todd.

He didn't deserve her but there was something between them that neither of them could ignore.

He hoped it wasn't all in his imagination. He knew he loved her more than he'd ever loved anyone in his life and if she'd only give him another chance he'd do anything to share his life with her.

Or was he jumping to impossible conclusions?

She wasn't just Kelly, she was also Jasmine James, and could probably have any man she set her sights on. Why should he think she felt as he did? They weren't on holiday any longer, this was real life.

He gave an involuntary sigh as he paid the taxi driver.

It had been a very enjoyable evening but she had told her mother they were just good friends, hadn't she? He didn't want her friendship, though — it just wasn't enough. They'd started as friends and it had blossomed into love. That could happen but love couldn't revert to friendship, not for them. He knew that if he couldn't have her love he wouldn't be satisfied with only her friendship.

He'd left his car at her apartment so he might see her for a while tomorrow when he went to collect it. In the evening would be a good time, call in casually and try and assess the situation.

His last thought before he fell asleep was that he hoped he would have the opportunity to see her again tomorrow and how much he loved her.

★ ★ ★

Desmond didn't single her out for criticism next day Kelly was pleased to discover. He had spent weeks dishing out harsh remarks to everyone in turn but now he was spending the last few days encouraging and paying compliments to boost confidence. Without exception, they were all word perfect, the dance routines were faultless, not a flat note in the singing. Yes, there was a certain air of trepidation as the first night approached but that was to be expected.

Zara had left her a salad and cold meat with a note to tell her that she would be dining with Todd. That meant that unless David simply drove off without getting in touch she would have the chance to see him on her own.

Kelly spent her time while she waited in going over the script again. She wasn't sure whether she was more nervous of her performance on the first night or of seeing David on her own. Both were fraught with a certain amount of anxiety and a great deal of anticipated excitement.

When her mobile rang she was trying out the steps of the opening number. She snatched it up and when it was David telling her he was on his way to collect his car she was elated.

'I'll look forward to seeing you then.'

She smiled. 'Mum's left me cold roast beef and a salad so if you haven't eaten we could share it.'

'Sounds great. Do you want me to bring anything?'

'No.' *Just bring yourself,* she thought, feeling quite light headed at seeing him so soon.

She sat by the intercom waiting for him to arrive and when he did, pressed the button for him to enter.

'Come in,' Kelly whispered shyly when he reached her door.

'It's good to see you,' he replied as though they hadn't seen each other for years and they both laughed.

'I hoped you wouldn't just pick up your car and drive off,' she admitted.

He followed her into the lounge. 'Hardly! All I could think of all day was seeing you again. How's the show going?'

'All right, hopefully.'

'That's good.'

'Shall we eat?'

'If you're sure you don't mind sharing.'

His blue eyes were fixed on her and she felt mesmerised. 'No, not at all,' she whispered.

'Kelly? Dare I think . . . '

She didn't know who made the first move but she was in his arms and he was holding her close like she had longed for him to do. Their meal was forgotten as his lips fastened on to hers.

'I've dreamed of this moment,' he told her softly, 'but I didn't think it could happen. I love you so very much, I can't think of anything else.'

'I'm so happy when I'm with you David. I want you to know that while I have the courage to tell you. There's just one thing that really troubles me.'

He ran his hand gently over her hair as she rested her head on his shoulder. 'I know it could be difficult with you being so committed to being in *Smiling Through Tears* but I want you to believe that I do fully understand the situation and will do everything in my power to accommodate it. Being in the show is an important part of your life and I accept that I will have to share you with your fans but I hope that one day I can be the person you come home to and that will be more than good enough for me.'

'Are you saying . . . '

He kissed the top of her head. 'I'm saying I will love you forever and will you marry me?'

'I will!' she cried ecstatically and she lifted her head and stretched up to kiss him.

'One day,' he promised, 'we will go back to Tunisia and see all the places we didn't see last time. I would like to say we'll go for our honeymoon but I accept that with the show being so new you won't be able to get the time off.'

'I'm sorry, I suppose it depends how long away the marriage is.'

'From my point of view as soon as it can be arranged.'

'From my point of view that sounds perfect,' she agreed.

It was then she thought of Jan and

what she'd been about to say before David interrupted.

'And now,' David continued with a grin, 'how about that food you mentioned earlier?'

She'd question him about Jan later. 'It's all ready. There's some more beef in the fridge and a fresh loaf of crusty bread so you won't starve. I still have the spices you bought me. When we're married I'll make you some really interesting meals with them, just you wait and see.'

'I could live on beans on toast,' he told her, 'just as long as you are there, Kelly.'

'One day I might remind you of that,' she teased.

He kissed her very gently. 'I'll even open the tin for you.'

She laughed as though he had come out with the funniest remark ever. As they ate their meal she thought again about Jan and some of her happiness disappeared.

He spread butter thickly on to his

bread. 'You're looking suddenly worried. Are you having second thoughts about a quick marriage?'

She shook her head.

'It's not that. I don't know how Jan will take the news when I tell her.'

He looked puzzled. 'Are you saying Jan doesn't like me? I would have said Jan and I got on really well.'

'That's just it, David. If she loves you as well, she's going to be so upset. And your mother will be too. I understand she gets on well with her. To be honest, I had the impression that Jan was practically one of the family.'

'Me and Jan?' He almost choked. 'You surely didn't think there was anything going on between Jan and me! Yes, Jan does get on well with my mother as you pointed out, and yes, I do believe that my mother would be happy to have her as a daughter-in-law, but Jan knows it's you I love.'

'So how can your mother think she might one day be her daughter-in-law?' she asked.

David smiled. 'Because, my darling, my mother has two sons and it is Simon who is interested in Jan. I asked Jan if she would visit my mother to do her hair at Sally's suggestion. She met Simon when he was home from working in Afghanistan. It seems we are not the only ones to experience love at first sight.'

'That never occurred to me! A few minutes ago I thought I was as happy as I could ever be but I am even happier now. I hated the possibility of bad feelings between Jan and me.'

11

Friday was the opening night of the show. Jan had arrived that morning and Kelly went over to the hotel to see her. Simon was there too as was her future mother-in-law.

'Fancy me being related to Jasmine James,' she chortled. 'I thought my boys would never get married and here we are talking weddings for both of them. Just shows you never know what tomorrow is going to bring.'

Jan raised her champagne glass. 'Let's drink to health, wealth and happiness,' she toasted.

'And love,' Kelly added, her eyes shining.

Sally and Leo turned up not much later, Sally already wearing a smock to show off her pregnancy.

David had managed to get a couple of hours off and arrived not long after

Sally and Leo. They were looking forward to the show and Kelly prayed it would all go smoothly.

David drove her back to her apartment and suggested she have a rest.

'I can't. I'm too wound up. I'm terrified and excited. I don't want to let anyone down, particularly Desmond. He's acting full of confidence but it is an act. You never know how the audience will react, not to mention the critics who'll be there.'

'Well if they all start to boo, our little party will stand up and cheer,' he promised her with a grin. 'Don't worry; I'm sure it will be great.'

He kissed her lingeringly and left her at her apartment.

★ ★ ★

Kelly could feel herself literally shaking as she waited in the wings to go on stage. She was dressed in a drab grey skirt and a short navy coat, far removed from the glamorous gear that Jasmine

173

James was famous for. This was Jasmine James as no one had ever seen her before and there was a hushed silence as she joined the dancers in the opening number and then there she was centre stage and all alone. Her trembling had disappeared and the thrill of playing to a packed theatre took over. She forgot everything as she poured out her heart, her voice soft at first and then hitting the high notes with exquisite ease.

As the number came to a close there was spontaneous applause.

During the interval Desmond came to her dressing room. 'You were good at rehearsals, Jasmine, but an audience lifts you to another level.'

'Thank you,' she replied humbly.

'I've heard on the grapevine that you're thinking of getting married. He's a very lucky man.' He kissed her cheek. 'Congratulations.'

'Thank you,' she repeated, this time with a smile.

'I don't expect you to take time off,' he warned.

'Don't worry, we've already discussed that.'

'Good,' he said. 'I have a feeling this is going to be my biggest hit yet.'

He was right.

* * *

'Good morning my beautiful wife,' David whispered as he placed a cup of tea on the bedside table.

'Mmm,' she murmured sleepily.

'I'm off to work,' he told her. 'I'll see you later.'

She forced her eyes open and sat up. 'I can't believe we're actually married. Not everyone gets married in a registry office and then goes on to do a matinee.'

'You said you wanted a very quiet wedding,' he reminded her. 'Are you regretting it?'

'Not at all!' She stretched out her arms invitingly. 'Where's my cuddle?'

'Darling, are you trying to make me late for work?' he said teasingly.

'Yes,' she said simply. 'It is our honeymoon. A rather unusual honeymoon with you at a critical stage of your new factory project and me doing eight shows a week.'

'When you are allowed some time off I promise we'll have a wonderful delayed honeymoon anywhere in the world.'

Her reply was immediate. 'Tunisia. We have so much to see. For now I'm satisfied being here in your flat. Our life will be one long honeymoon.'

'I'll have to go, sweetheart.' He kissed her again. 'I'm coming to see the show tonight so I'll be there to bring you home.'

'I won't expect you to be there every night.'

'See you later.'

She was married. It was unbelievable but true. Only her family and a few close friends knew about it. She'd worn a new cream two-piece suit with a pink blouse and a cluster of cream and pink imitation flowers in her hair. After the ceremony there had been an early lunch and then Kelly had gone on to the theatre.

Three of the girls in the chorus were taking over the lease of her flat. It had been one mad rush but she and David couldn't wait to be married once the decision had been made.

It was certainly a different wedding. The guests had all been given tickets to the show and they sat with David in the audience sharing their secret, keeping the media at bay for once.

* * *

True to his word David was at the theatre when the curtain went up. He'd brought his partner Jake with him and also the managing director of the new factory they were working on, together with his wife. Kelly thought her mother was right and whatever the obstacles love would always find a way.

At the end of the performance amidst the loud applause Desmond . Drake appeared on stage and raised his hand for quiet. Then he informed the surprised audience that Jasmine James had slipped out one day and got married. He called for the groom to come forward and David, looking rather bemused, had gone on to the stage.

Then he'd asked for Kelly to step forward and smiling at them both had quipped, 'You may kiss the bride.'

David readily obliged and everyone on stage and in the audience clapped and cheered before the curtain came down.

'You're a very secretive girl, Jasmine,' Desmond chastised her. 'It's a good thing I have big ears and overheard a couple of the girls talking about taking over your flat.'

'I need some privacy occasionally,' she protested.

'You can forget that. The news of your marriage will spread like wildfire.'

It didn't take long for Jasmine James to hit the headlines once more.

'Listen to this.' David, still in his dressing gown, had picked up the papers that had been delivered. 'NO TIME FOR A HONEYMOON. JASMINE JAMES, STAR OF SMILING THROUGH TEARS, MARRIES IN HER LUNCH BREAK. I'm getting a taste of what it's like to be a celebrity.'

David grimaced as he put down the newspapers on top of the duvet.

'Do you mind terribly?' Kelly asked anxiously.

'It feels a little bit odd but I'll just have to get used to it. I'm the lucky guy who gets to spend time alone with you.'

'It's hard to believe that we are actually married. In some ways it would have been nice to have had a white dress and all the trimmings but I liked it not being turned into a publicity event.'

'It was wonderful,' David said, 'and you looked divine. It was lovely in its own way, just your family and mine and a few close friends. I got to meet your dad and his wife. I must say he and your mum seemed to be on good speaking terms.'

'They've been divorced a long time. They've gone their separate ways and now Mum is officially engaged to Todd I think it's made it better.' Kelly became suddenly serious. 'We won't ever get divorced, will we David?'

'What a question to ask your new husband!' He matched her seriousness. 'To answer that, no we won't. We'll disagree sometimes, of course we will, we're still individuals but I hope we'll always be able to talk things through in the future.'

'You'll be late for work if you're not careful.'

'I've actually taken the whole day off.'

'Fantastic!' she giggled and moved in the bed to make room for him . . .

* * *

Two years had gone by in which time Sally had a little girl and Simon and Jan had got married.

Smiling Through Tears was a sell-out at the box office and David and Jake seemed to be making it in their architectural practice. Desmond had agreed to Kelly taking a fortnight's holiday much to the delight of her talented understudy.

'She's really good,' Kelly admitted to David. 'I hope this will be her chance to shine.'

They were back in Tunisia for a very delayed honeymoon and this time every day was packed with sightseeing.

'I take it you don't mind handing over the leading role to someone else?' David questioned.

'Not at all. I have other plans.'

'Desmond has another project planned for you?' asked David resignedly.

They'd been to Matmata with its cave dwellers, they'd visited the ancient city of Tozeur with its fascinating style of buildings. David was a mine of information and told her that it was an immense oasis irrigated by 200 springs, the water distributed by a system established in the 13th century. Kelly was thrilled to discover date palms contrasting with the dry soil and climate which derived their water from the inexhaustible springs.

They had seen so much and there was still so much to see.

Every day had been magical but today was the one Kelly would remember for the rest of her life. They were on a two-day safari and David was grumbling about getting up so early.

'It will be worth it,' Kelly told him excitedly. 'If you want to see the sunrise in the desert you can't go in the afternoon, can you?'

They were given warm clothing to wear in traditional style to combat the chill of the desert before the later heat.

'You were right, Kelly,' David said. 'Being on a camel and watching the sunrise is not something you can do every day. I can't imagine anything more wonderful.'

'Oh, I can,' she told him mysteriously. 'My new project as you put it . . . ' She smiled contentedly and chose that moment to tell him they were going to have a baby.

THE END

Other titles in the
Linford Romance Library:

TERESA'S TREASURE

Valerie Holmes

Teresa, as a child, dreamt of the day when the secret inside a tin box would be revealed to her. However, as she grows into a young woman her life changes dramatically, shattering her childhood dreams . . . yet she still remembers her treasure. Risking a possible marriage match, Teresa decides to go on a journey of discovery to seek it out. But some secrets are meant to stay buried. What she discovers is of greater value than she had ever imagined.

THE SHOWMAN'S GIRL

Julia Douglas

When Emily runs away with the circus in the 1930s, she enters a magical world of perilous adventures, intense friendships and deep passions. Growing up in the big top, she admires, from afar, the charismatic showman, Adam Strand. But Adam is torn between his wife Jayne, a daredevil tight-wire walker, and Molly, the elephant trainer who's always carried a torch for him. Emily becomes a star — but will she ever be able to tell Adam how she really feels?